"Very thought-provoking in its attempt to show what prejudice is and how people act who are caught in its web of misunderstanding. The story is told with a verve and humor that keep it from being in any way moralizing, although the author's message comes through clear and true."—Chicago *Tribune*

"All the misadventures of transplanting from city sidewalks to suburban folkways are recounted with a direct comic vision which enhances the book's major point without reducing its serious intent." (Starred Review)—*Kirkus Reviews*

"It is refreshing to read a book about anti-Semitism that sweeps nothing under the carpet, yet has humor, good characterization, good dialogue, and good style." (Recommended)—*Bulletin of the Center for Children's Books*

"Honesty and an effortless style distinguish this story."—*Commonweal*

BERRIES GOODMAN

BERRIES GOODMAN

by

Emily Cheney Neville

A HARPER TROPHY BOOK

HARPER & ROW, PUBLISHERS

NEW YORK, EVANSTON, SAN FRANCISCO, LONDON

Standard Book Number: 06–440072–7
First printed in 1965. 6th printing, 1974.
First Trophy edition.

To F. H. G.

Contents

1. Drives 1

2. The Country Estate 7

3. We Break It In, and Vice Versa 20

4. Neighbors 37

5. Friend 53

6. Mother's Outing 71

7. Mavis 88

8. Passover 99

9. Lyle 108

10. Accident 114

11. All That Trouble 124

12. Mothers 134

13. Bicycle 144

14. The Other Goodmans 158

15. New York 171

I

Drives

"New Jersey," Sidney said. "How do you get to New Jersey?"

"Through the tunnel," I said.

"Stupid, I know how you go with your family. You get in the car and your mom starts sputtering, 'Quiet now, all of you, I'm hunting for Route Three.' What I mean is, how do I get there with my"—Sidney pulled out his wallet and peered in—"three dollars and eighty-three cents? It'll be three-seventy-three after I pay for this Coke."

"I'll pay for your Coke. After all, you're my long-lost pal that I haven't seen since the olden times in Olcott Corners. That must be six years ago. Listen, why do you want to go to New Jersey, anyway?"

"Because I'm not going home! Boy, it almost kills me. This kid, Jeff, and I had tickets for the track meet and wrestling and a guitar guy at Carnegie Hall. We planned this weekend for ages."

"Did you tell your mom?"

"Well, I told her the general idea quite a while ago, but I didn't tell her the exact date, because then she'd spend all the time thinking up objections. Yesterday I told her, and she said, 'It's out of the question. You have to be home for the holiday. Grandfather is coming.' Creep, it isn't a real important holiday."

"Can't you talk her into it? You know, really put on the heat?"

"Nah. Mom heats up worse than I do." Sidney poked at his ice cubes with the wilted straw and then spun around on the counter stool as if he'd like to fly off into space. "I could just call up and tell her I was staying at Jeff's. She couldn't do anything. But after all, she's my mother, and everything."

"Won't she be just as mad if you go to New Jersey?"

"Not exactly. It's part of my family, and Mom figures a holiday has got to be a family day. My brother lives in New Jersey—you remember Marty. He'll call Mom up and smooth her down. I really like Marty's wife. I like to visit them."

"I'm about ready to go somewhere myself," I said.

"This being at high school at home gets to be a drag. I want to go to college out west, like Utah, maybe."

"Utah! What's out there?"

"My dad came from there. He says it's pretty nice. Listen, how come you moved away from Olcott?"

"Mom got some idea the school out there wasn't good enough to get me into a top college. Then my father died, and she wanted to be closer to her relatives in New York, so we moved into Hastings and I go to a really tough school. I like it all right. Jeff—that's my friend—is nothing like me. He's bright enough to get by in school, but he's mostly interested in sports and cars. His parents are divorced, and they don't fuss any about holidays and relatives. Mom's sort of suspicious of him —she thinks he's a bad influence on me or something."

"Like I used to be, out in Olcott?"

Sidney wrinkled up his forehead, thinking. Finally he said, "No, that was different. You were . . . oh, I don't know. Listen, if I'm going to make this break for freedom, I better find out about the buses."

"You get them at the Port Authority building. It's just a few blocks over. Come on, I'll show you." I paid for the Cokes and we started walking.

"How'd you find my phone number, anyway?" I asked, as we walked along Forty-second Street. "Once I looked you up in a phone book, but there were no Fines left in Olcott."

3

"I remembered your father's name, and there are two Dan Goodmans in the Manhattan book. I woke the other up, and he snarled at me, and then I got you. I meant to call you a lot of other times, but then somehow I always put it off."

"I know, like getting a haircut."

"Today I knew was the day. Boy, was I mad! I just had to talk to someone, and Jeff wouldn't understand. Even though he's my best friend, and we're probably going to college together."

"Where're you going?"

"Harvard, maybe. Except he may not get in."

I laughed. "How about you?"

Sidney looked a little puzzled that I should ask. He wasn't boasting; he just said as a fact, "I'll get in. How about you—who does your math now?"

"I do my own, and I pass. And I'll have you know I'm in an honor English class and Mr. McHarry, who's the teacher of it, thinks I'm a raving genius."

"Find the bus for Oradell, genius," Sidney said as we walked into the terminal. I took him to the upper level, which is a madhouse with about three hundred commuter buses going to three hundred different places in New Jersey.

I could tell Sidney didn't know much about bus terminals because while he was buying his ticket he asked the girl if the bus stopped near Spruce Street,

4

where his brother lived. She hardly looked up as she reeled off: "Ask the driver. Next bus is the four forty-nine, gate one-o-three. Round trip?"

"Oh, uh, no," Sidney stuttered. "One way."

The girl looked up, deadpan, and said, "We're sure going to miss you."

Sidney didn't get it at first; then he started blushing. I took him to the gate and it was almost four forty-nine and suddenly we had nothing to say. He threw his coat over his shoulder and walked through. He half turned to wave.

"So long!" I said. It sure seemed a casual way to say good-bye to a guy I hadn't seen in half a dozen years. When he was almost out of sight, Sidney turned and shouted something, but I couldn't hear.

I walked home. It's funny in New York how you can walk for blocks, stopping at traffic lights and even reading signs and looking in windows without really hardly noticing them at all. I walked through the districts for wholesale flowers, Greek restaurants, and on down to carnival goods and toys. All the time I was thinking about seeing Sidney again and wondering what he was going to prove in New Jersey.

Drives, that's what my teacher Mr. McHarry is always talking about. He says people do things because of drives, like love and hate and hunger and fear. He

5

doesn't count things like being grouchy because of a headache.

So what's Sidney's drive, going to New Jersey, I wonder? Obviously, because he's mad at his mother. I try to remember what his mother looked like. Before we had all that trouble, I thought she was really a nice mother.

I'm crossing Broadway at Twenty-third Street, under the Flatiron Building, and I stop on the island. I can't remember Mrs. Fine's face, but all of a sudden I can remember Mrs. Graham, Sandra's mother. She's saying, "It's unfortunate, of course. Sidney just wasn't as able."

Standing in the middle of Broadway, after missing the traffic light, I can almost feel again the hot rush of rage, mixed with fear that I might cry. I guess that was the only time in my life I was ever thoroughly, totally, angry. Angry at that Mrs. Graham, Sandra's mother. That's the kind of thing McHarry means by a drive.

But here I am—I finish crossing Broadway and go on toward Seventeenth Street—and Sidney's the one who's popping off to New Jersey to prove something, or find something. So how do you figure that out?

2

The Country Estate

Olcott Corners was the name of the place where I knew Sidney. It's a suburb about fifty miles out of New York. To begin with, though, my family lived right in New York. They had this little apartment on East Fifty-first Street, that my father had before he was even married, when there was just him and Yogi Berra, a cocker spaniel.

Then there was Mom, and Dad, and Yogi; then my older brother, Hal; eight years later, me, Bertrand, known as Berries. Seven years later came the disaster, Jennifer.

Mom and Dad were so used to the apartment and the neighborhood that they didn't think of moving when

Jennifer was born, and not for quite a while after. They put a crib in the front hall for her, right handy for dumping your coat on. Mom and Dad slept on a convertible bed in the living room, and Hal and I shared the bedroom. About all I remember is him yelling all the time that I'd crayoned in his notebook, or wrecked his best model, and that he didn't have any place to do his homework. Finally he got a board to put across the basin in the bathroom, and he used to lock himself in there to work.

Hal is very resourceful, I'll have to admit, even though he is a pain in the neck sometimes. He's the only one who tries to keep things organized in this family.

Mom is quite efficient, but only in waves, when she's got a new project. Between projects everything slumps: Mantelpieces pile up, socks get holes, tuna fish gets more often. You might think that girls learn to be motherly by having children, but this doesn't seem to be so: They're either born that way or they're not. Mom's not. She's least of all motherly about Jennifer.

I guess Dad is fatherly; anyway he likes children, his own or anyone else's. He's an editor at *Young Lady* magazine, and he's always reading and writing and correcting stuff, but he forgets to put gas in the car and he doesn't know how to make the faucets stop dripping. Hal always used to get the washers and put them in.

Now our faucets just drip, because Hal has been at college and then in the Navy.

When Jennifer was about two years old, she learned how to get out of the crib, and she learned it at five o'clock one Sunday morning. That was when Mom decided we should move, and she went into one of her efficient cycles. By the time the rest of us got up that Sunday morning, she had read the entire *New York Times* real estate section.

But without much success. Apartments were very hard to find, and Mom was determined to stay right in the same neighborhood. She's shy about making new friends, and she'd gone to the same drugstore and laundry for twenty years, and we practically *lived* on pastrami and pickles from Glotz's Delicatessen next door. All the apartments available, though, were in new buildings and cost about three times as much rent as our old one.

Mom kept right on getting up early with Jennifer and cleaning and throwing things away, and Dad complained that he was all tired out before he even went to work. We'd always been a late-sleeping family, because Dad goes to work late. Hal had always kept the alarm clock and got me up and tossed Jennifer her first bottle, so this daybreak rising was quite a shock to Dad.

Finally Dad started looking at the real estate section too. But he started with the Farms and Acreage section, because he's always talked about this "back to the earth" business; eventually he worked down to suburban real estate.

"I'll bet we can rent a house in the country as cheaply as we can rent one of these fancy apartments," he said.

Mom said, "What country?"

Hal said, "Where'll I go to school?"

I said, "Yippee! I'll get a new bike and a dog!"

For some reason no one pointed out that the suburbs were well out of the East Fifty-first Street neighborhood, or that Dad would have to go on getting up at daybreak to catch a train in to work.

The next weekend, a new way of life began. Dad remembered to get the car greased and full of gas, and we set off for the country to look at houses. Jennifer got left home with a strange baby-sitter, which was a rude shock in her young life. Before, Mom had just left her with Hal occasionally. Every time she saw a sitter, Jennifer started screaming, and she was usually still at it when we came back. A very stubborn sort of baby.

Finding a house did not turn out to be much easier than finding an apartment, at least not one anyone liked that we could also afford. Most of them were for sale, not for rent, and Mom and Dad kept doing mental arithmetic about mortgages. Hal had pocketfuls of old envelopes covered with figuring, to show them where they'd multiplied wrong.

We went past plenty of nifty houses that I liked, with clean paint and neat little fenced yards for a dog, but Mom and Dad wouldn't even look at them. Dad wanted a house with a big, wild sort of backyard—but within five minutes of the railway station. No one knew what Mom wanted. Half the times she walked out of places in disgust, I think it was because she didn't like the looks of the people or their furniture. Of course *they'd* move out if *we* moved in, but she forgot that.

Every weekend we saw about one place that might be possible. As we drove home, they argued about it. By the next weekend they'd decided No, and we set out again. New baby-sitter (the same one never came again), more screams from Jennifer. Hal liked it because he could drive the car, once we were outside the city. He was seventeen that year and not allowed to drive in New York.

One extra-hot Sunday in the middle of June we set off, and I had a friend along, Irvy Weinstein. His father owns a kosher bakery, and Irvy brought along a whole bagful of fresh bagels and bialys and also that sticky apricot candy they call shoeleather. The sweaty hot day and the shoeleather combined to make me and Irvy

11

pretty smudgy looking by the time Hal turned off the parkway. He drove on to Village Real Estate in a small town named Olcott Corners.

Some of the real estate people are pretty nice, but some of them talk all the time, probably figuring you'll buy a house to shut them up and get away. The lady we hit was that kind.

She got in the front seat with Mom and Hal, and Dad climbed in back with us. Miss Real Estate let her eyes flicker over me and Irvy, and then resolutely turned to snow Mom under with words.

"You want something nice and modern, of course. Sunny and cheerful. So nice for the children after the city, I suppose they can hardly wait. You have a baby, too? How nice! A really modern house can save you so much work."

She half turned to include Dad in the conversation, and Irvy took the opportunity to offer her a slightly soiled bagel.

"Mmm, a pretzel, how nice. Not just now, thank you."

"It's not a pretzel; it's a bagel. His pop makes them," I said. I was quite surprised when she left her mouth half open and stared, first at me and Irvy and then at Dad.

Dad nodded politely. "It *is* a bagel. Perhaps you'd like one of the other kind. They're bialys. Don't mind

12

Berries here. He just likes to correct everyone."

"Of course," said Miss Real Estate and closed her mouth. Her eyes sort of glazed over and she dived into this book she was carrying around, and then she came out again and said, "Now, if you'll take the next left, young man, there are several *darling* houses I can show you."

The darling houses were in a development called Olcott Acres, and I thought they were neat. There were lots of kids and bikes around, and the houses were brand new and I bet they had push-button everything.

Hal slowed down, but Mom said, "I don't think this is quite what we want."

"A few more real—uh, acres," said Dad.

"They never like anything good," I groaned to Irvy.

Miss Real Estate smiled bravely and directed Hal down Indian Road. There were some houses with apple orchards and brooks, and Dad was nuts about them, but when he heard the price he said, "Back to town, Hal."

Olcott Corners is quite an old village, with a genuine village green. There are four churches around it, and one soda shop. Dad told Hal to slow down, so he could look at the old churches. Smiling innocently, he asked Miss Real Estate, "You don't have a Mormon church, do you?"

People are apt to think Dad is kidding about

13

Mormons, but as a matter of fact, he was born in Provo, Utah, and his people were Mormons, and Dad's been swimming in Great Salt Lake.

While Miss Real Estate was trying to collect her thoughts, I got a little worried about Dad studying the churches.

"Listen, Dad, you know you said I don't have to go to Sunday school in the country, unless I decide to myself. You said I could get a *dog*."

I guess the way I said it, I sounded as if I was trading a used Sunday school for a new model dog.

Miss Real Estate sort of stared at me again. I didn't know what was bothering her, but I could tell she was making a big fake of trying to seem very casual when she asked me, "What Sunday school do you usually go to, dear?"

"There's no 'usually' about it. I go to Turtle Bay Community Church."

Dad explained: "You see, Berr—that is, Bertrand —joined the swimming club, the checkers club, and the Cub Scouts at this church, so I said it was only fair for him to attend the main event too. I'm a Mormon myself, but I'm broadminded."

Miss Real Estate gulped. "Maybe Bertrand will change his mind about attending one of our lovely churches."

"Any of them have swimming pools?" I asked.

14

Mom was getting restless. "Are there any more *houses,* not too expensive, that we could see?"

Miss Real Estate suddenly turned on a really radiant, push-button smile and started whizzing through the pages of her real estate book again.

"This might be *just* the thing! Moderate priced too. I can't think how I forgot it. It's out on the other side of town, but you won't mind a short drive. I can see this young man is a born driver. This house is most un . . . uh, uh . . . usual."

The house was unusual, all right. The front door opened into a big rhododendron bush, but it hadn't been opened in years. The usable entrance was into the kitchen, and almost the whole rest of the kitchen wall was a big plate glass window. This intrigued Mom, who would a whole lot rather look out a window than cook. This window overlooked a big yard, sort of bumpy and shaggy, sloping down to a garage at one corner and up to a tree with a treehouse in it at the other.

"Yipes, come on, Irvy!" I yelled, and we took title to the treehouse. Mom and Hal went into the house with Miss Real Estate, but Dad started walking down past the garage. I looked that way and there was a little pond.

"Wow! This place has everything!" Irvy and I followed him. We walked all around the pond, which was absolutely jumping with polliwogs.

15

"Say, this is quite a spot," said Dad. "We could get a rowboat and have picnics down here and . . ."

"Whyn't you build a barbecue?" Irvy asked.

"I got to get a jar to put polliwogs in," I said.

I went up to the house and found Mom sitting on a funny little half flight of stairs that came down into the kitchen. She was just sitting there smoking. Hal and Miss Real Estate had gone into the cellar.

"You know where they keep the jars around here?"

"No," Mom said. "Look, Berries, there's a whole big bathroom up here, just by itself at the top of these little stairs. I could go in and lock the door and no one could get *at* me!"

"Neat," I said. "Any old jars in it?"

"Try the utility room." Mom made a face and added, "That's what *she* calls it. It's right under the bathroom and it has the washing machine and stuff in it."

"Is it one of those big automatic jobs—is it, Mom?"

"I don't think so. It looks old."

Mom hasn't much sense about machines. Even now, she let a guy sell her a bargain model with no filter trap, so every time a penny gets caught in the drain, you have to pay a repairman eight bucks to get it out.

The machine in the utility room was not just old.

16

It was antique and rusted. I did find some old mason jars on a shelf, though, and I was just starting back to the pond when Hal and Miss Real Estate came up from the cellar.

She rattled along: "Now, upstairs there are four lovely bedrooms, and you're simply going to *adore* the closet space!"

Mom said, "It's the bathroom I like."

Hal and I raced for the bedrooms, to see who could get fins on the best one. Hal said the big one over the kitchen had to be for Mom and Dad. I was standing in the next to biggest one, and Hal looked it all over and then he shrugged and said I could have it. Miss Real Estate was sure right about the closets. The one in my room was big enough to build a fort in. Mom came and looked at all the bedrooms too, and then we went down. Dad and Irvy came back from the pond.

Mom said, "Dan, I think this is really *it*, don't you?"

"Yeah, it's nice. Come on, you've got to see the pond."

Hal said, "Look, Dad, I think it's great, too, but you got to look at the *house*. I mean, for instance, the roof leaks. Up in Berries' room."

That's why he let me have it. I told you—Hal always figures the angles.

"And there's something wrong with the water pres-

17

sure. Look, it hardly runs here." Hal turned on the kitchen faucet, which dribbled.

Miss Real Estate picked up with a rush. "The house is really in excellent condition. There are always a few little things with a house that's been . . . unoccupied."

"It hasn't been exactly selling like hotcakes, hmm?" Dad asked. When it comes right down to parting with money, he's not as vague as he makes out.

Miss Real Estate spun him a long improbable tale about a family whose children and grandmother all got sick just as they were about to pay forty-five thousand for the place.

"We certainly couldn't go that high," Dad said. "In fact since the place has been vacant for so long, perhaps the owner would consider a lease. You know, for two or three years. Till we see how the Goodmans and the country get along together."

Miss Real Estate's face crumpled. She looked like a little girl whose ice cream pop just fell off the stick. Bravely she tried to pull up her lower lip.

"Mr. Hayes never said anything about a rental."

"Maybe he never thought of it," said Dad. "Let's just suggest it to him."

"Don't you want me to show you around the—uh, house? You haven't seen the cellar."

Mom stood up and snapped her pocketbook shut

the way she does when she's just made up her mind.

"No, the house is fine. We like it. Let's go talk to the man about the price."

Later, when Mom went to work, we found out all about commissions on real estate. A salesman doesn't make much on a rental, which of course is why Miss Real Estate was so disappointed at our talking about renting, instead of buying. Down at the real estate office she phoned the owner, and you could tell from her voice she wasn't trying very hard to persuade him.

Dad got on the phone himself, and first thing you know he and Mr. Hayes—that was the owner—were talking about magazines and then about beefsteak tomatoes. The upshot of it was that Mr. Hayes said he'd talk to his lawyer about rental payments applying to later purchase of the house, and meantime Dad could put down a deposit so they wouldn't sell the house while everyone made up their minds.

Everyone looked happy, except Miss Real Estate, who gingerly accepted Dad's check. He recapped his dime-store pen and said, "In twenty-three months, kids, we may be the proud and mortgaged owners of a trout pond and country estate, complete with antique roof dating back to Revolutionary days."

3

We Break It In,
and Vice Versa

During the next couple of weeks, Mom dashed around making new decisions every half hour. At eight o'clock every morning she called Mr. Hayes to find out if he had agreed to renting. At the end of a week he broke down —I guess he was sick of having his breakfast interrupted—and said we could rent the house for two years for two hundred and fifty dollars a month. If we notified him that we wanted to buy the house at the end of the first year, we could apply the rent against the purchase price.

Dad went out to sign the lease the next weekend, and I got to go with him. Mom kept Hal home to help her pack. I thought I was getting a big treat, but at the last minute Hal shoved Jennifer off on us. She practically ruined my whole day.

Mom gave Dad a long list of all the things she wanted Mr. Hayes to fix at the house. Most of them he forgot. Jennifer fell half in the pond and she was all muddy, and I had to keep chasing her around the yard. Dad was busy talking gardens with Mrs. Hayes. I looked up and saw this girl with pigtails, a couple of years older than me, leaning on the fence smirking. I looked pretty silly, chasing a muddy baby around. The girl didn't say anything, and neither did I, but that was my first sight of Sandra.

Mom went right on phoning Mr. Hayes about the things that needed fixing all the next week. One day, before she had time to say anything, he told her that we were responsible for keeping the lawn mowed. She stopped phoning him so much after that.

Hal heard about the lawn, and he tackled Dad. "What kind of a lawnmower have we got? I forgot to look in the garage."

Dad was sorting out back copies of his magazine. "The ordinary kind. It has a wooden handle and blades that go round."

Hal groaned. "No motor. Look, Dad, most of that lawn is on the side of a hill."

"I knew it," said Mom. "Now you'll want to buy a new power mower, and I'll have to go on washing diapers in the bathtub instead of getting a new washing machine that works."

"But you'll hang them out in the sun-dappled country air, with the wind caressing your hair. Look, it says so right here." Dad pointed to a copy of *Young Lady*.

"Throw that one out," said Mom.

I realized finally that neither Mom or Dad really had any idea what it was like to live in a house in the suburbs. Mom had never lived in a house in her life. Sounds funny, I know, but she grew up in Brooklyn in an apartment, and she says she came to Manhattan because she thought with her beautiful auburn hair she could make her fortune as an actress. She couldn't. She lived in a tiny apartment with two other girls and worked in an office, until she married Dad.

Dad has sort of a lean, western look, like the good guys on TV, but not quite that handsome. He doesn't look, or act, like an industrious suburban homeowner. I guess he must have lived in a house out in Utah, but it wasn't anything like Olcott, and it's so long ago he's pretty much forgotten it. He only remembers the places he learned to hide in to get out of doing chores.

Hal had visited friends in the suburbs, so at least he knew about lawnmowers and the mad morning rush for the train. Hal has always had a good lot of friends to invite him to things. He's tall and looks something like Dad, except he has reddish-brown hair like Mom's. I've got freckles and pumpkin-colored hair on a pump-kin-shaped head.

We fumbled up to moving day, all pretty ignorant. It seemed to take the movers hours to get us loaded, and then Mom and us kids drove out to the house and waited hours for them to come. Of course we didn't have much of anything with us for lunch. This was the beginning of the great hungry period in my life.

The movers just finished unloading in time for Mom to get Dad from the early train, which he had promised to take so he could help unpack and also pay the movers. He paid them and he said that just about cleaned him out.

That and the delicatessen. It was a lucky thing he had realized there might be a famine in the country, and he had really brought along a lot of goodies—pastrami, olive salad, three kinds of cheese, bagels, cake, and halvah bars. It was the last homey meal I had for a long time.

After dinner Mom put Jennifer to bed and we got to work unpacking. People kept handing me great stacks of books or shoes or sheets to carry upstairs. Finally Mom handed me some saucepans to put in the kitchen. I put them there and eased quietly out the back door.

It was pretty nice outside at night in the country—

moon and trees, and everything reflected in the pond. Most nights in the city I never got outside when the moon was up. I strolled toward the pond, feeling very nature-loving, except that I began to smell a very bad smell, not blossoms and grass at all, at all.

I stepped off the driveway tentatively. The ground was all squshy. I took about two steps, but it only got softer, and smellier. I got back on the road and sauntered down to the pond, which had a musky smell, but nice.

When I went back to the house, they seemed to have most of the boxes unpacked. Hal had taken off his shirt, and he was streaky with dust and sweat, putting books in the bookcase.

"Hey, Dad," I said, "you know that patch of lawn below the driveway, down toward the garage?"

"Yeah, we've got lots of patches."

"That particular patch, it stinks."

Hal threw a book at me. "Work, will you! Take that pile of trash out."

Dad said, "Yes, let's get this done. We can worry about how the lawn looks later."

"I didn't say how it *looked*," I said, but Hal just tossed some more junk at me. I took it outside and stayed out until Mom shouted it was time to go to bed.

In the city I always had to be waked up. That first

morning in Olcott I came to with the sun in my eyes and the birds making more noise than you would think a bunch of little bitty birds could make. I heard Jennifer sort of crying and singing, so I let her out and we went down into the kitchen. I dished us out some sugar-frosted flakes and milk, and after I'd thrown the carton away, I noticed there wasn't any more milk. I put the carton in the trash barrel outside.

Dad came trotting down the stairs next, whistling and chirping like a bird himself.

"Pretty nice getting up in the morning in the country, isn't it? What's for breakfast?"

"Nothing. Jen and I just had a little bit of cereal." I looked pathetic and hoped he would feel like going to the store for a coffee cake or something.

He boiled a little water for instant coffee and drank half of it. " 'Bye-bye. I'm going to grab the early train so I'll be home early. Tell Mom I'll try to be home by five, to help you pioneers settle."

I heard the car zoom off, and then I wondered how us pioneers were going to get to the store for supplies.

Mom and Hal came down, and Hal opened the icebox. "No milk!" he yelped.

"No milk," I agreed sadly.

Mom, who does not generally speak first thing in the morning, pointed to the instant coffee and a drawer she'd put the bread in. She put water on to boil. Hal went outside to look at the morning. Mom had lit her cigarette and started on her coffee, when he came back.

"You know that patch of lawn Berries was talking about?" he started. It is especially a mistake to ask Mom questions in the morning, so he hurried on: "Well, he was right, it does smell bad. The sewer pipe is leaking."

Mom took a big swallow of coffee, groaned, and ground out her cigarette. She walked outside in her bathrobe and bare feet. She came back and dialed a number on the telephone. It rang and rang.

Hal said, "It's rather early. I mean, it's not even seven yet."

"Not seven yet!" Mom stared at him. "What in the world am *I* doing up?"

"It's the birds," I said. "Dad left already. He said to tell you he'd be home early—five I think he said."

Mom howled. "He's left already? In the car?"

I nodded.

Mom groaned. She grabbed the nearest book out of a packing box and retreated up the stairs to her private bathroom and locked the door.

"What're we going to do for food?" I asked Hal.

He shrugged. "The stores won't even be open for about three hours, so we can think about it."

"*Think* about it! I'm already starving. If I'd known

26

they didn't have delicatessens in the country, I wouldn't of come."

We heard a crash of something tipping over and Jennifer crying upstairs, and Hal said, "Get your mind off your stomach and go see what's happened. Get dressed too."

I guessed I'd better stay in good with him if I expected to eat, so I went.

Jennifer came back downstairs with me, and she found her stroller and started wheeling it all around the house and trying to get out the back door with it.

Mom came in and stood looking at her. "I know; she thinks it's time to go to the park, poor thing, and here it is only eight o'clock."

"I saw an old playpen down in the garage," Hal said. "People I stayed with in the country all used to put their babies out in the yard in them. Come on, Berries."

We went and got it and wiped off some spiders and about a ton of dust. It smelled even worse down by the garage, now that the sun was up. We put the playpen up near the house and went and got our Jen. She stood in the center for one second and then threw herself down on her stomach and started drawing in her breath. When she had enough breath, she started screaming. Hal and I went indoors.

We shoved furniture around and helped Mom get

the rug down, which made us very thirsty. Mom made us drink warm boiled water, because she said we might catch typhoid from the water on account of the sewer leak. Did you ever drink warm boiled water when you were thirsty?

The phone rang. Mom answered, and listened, and said crossly, "Who is this?" She got an answer and said, "All right," and she hung up.

"The brat that lives next door thinks something is wrong with Jennifer. She's screaming. You'd better bring her in."

So now we had Jennifer underfoot. That must have been that girl with the pigtails I saw before. Busybody.

At nine o'clock Mom finally got Mr. Hayes on the phone and told him she was going to get the chief of police and the health department right away if he didn't do something about the sewer. He said he would, but he didn't seem to think it was nearly as important as Mom did.

"We could all come down with bubonic plague, and he wouldn't care!" Mom said. She started slamming pots and pans around and unpacking groceries, which would have been a hopeful sign, except there wasn't much but flour and spaghetti and that sort of stuff. There was some powdered milk, and Mom mixed it with boiled water and gave Jennifer a bottle and put her to bed. That was an improvement.

Hal unpacked two tiny cans of imported cheese and deviled ham that somebody had given us for Christmas once, and we put that on toast, and mixed the milk up with plenty of sugar and some coffee. Lunch, we called it. It wasn't even eleven o'clock yet.

Still, I felt better, and I went and arranged some models and baseball cards on my shelf and threw my shoes in the closet. I had four new pairs of socks, white with striped tops, and I put them in my top drawer and put all the old socks in the bottom drawer under my sweaters. Then the plumbers came, so I quit unpacking.

I don't know what language they spoke, but it was mostly grunts and they didn't tell us anything. Jennifer got up again and started whimpering.

I looked at Hal and said, "She needs food."

"Make toast," he said.

I put two pieces in. "That happens to be the last two pieces of bread," I said.

Jennifer ate a little toast, dropped the rest on the floor, and started whimpering again.

I munched on the other piece. "How far is it to town?"

"Couple of miles," Hal said.

"It's not really too far to walk."

"So, go ahead."

"I don't know the way."

Hal sat for a while, not saying anything, and I didn't bother him. Finally he said, "There's no use going, unless we can carry stuff home. Go get the stroller."

"Me?"

Hal said, "*I'm* sure not wheeling a stroller to town alone. Everyone'd think I was crazy."

"What'll they think I am?"

"Crazy." He smiled at me with brotherly love. "It's *your* stomach that's growling. Besides, I'll be there to protect you if anyone laughs."

"Huh." I thought it over for a while, but there didn't seem to be any way out, so I went and got the stroller.

In front of the house next door the girl with the pigtails was just waiting for us to wheel by. She dropped her ball in front of us, so we had to pause. While she picked it up she said, "Where's the baby?"

"Home," Hal said.

"Whyn't you take her in the carriage?" she asked.

"Because we're going to get groceries."

"In the *carriage?* Whyn't you take the car? Aren't you old enough to drive?"

"He's old enough, but Dad took the car," I said.

She bounced the ball a few times. "*We* have *two* cars," she said. "A Buick and a Chevy."

"How nice for you," said Hal. "Why didn't you do it right and get a Cadillac?"

"My Dad says they're cheap," said the girl.

"Cheap!" I yelped. "They cost about ten thousand dollars!"

"I don't mean *that* kind of cheap," she said. "I mean they're vulgar. The only people who drive them are—"

Hal pushed the stroller past her at this point, and I called over my shoulder, "You're really a feeb!" That was my newest insult.

Once you finally get to them, which we did in about half an hour, the country supermarkets are really jazzy, much bigger than the ones we had in New York.

Hal made us buy hamburger, which isn't so good if you forget the ketchup. He forgot the ketchup. I managed to throw into the basket some potato chips, a chocolate loaf cake, and a new kind of fruity sugared cereal. There was a free plastic rocket launcher in the box. What with milk and bread and sodas, that was about as much as we could carry in the stroller. We started the hot way home, uphill mostly.

Two little girls hanging out the back of a station wagon pointed at us and giggled. "Lookit the boys pushing groceries in a baby buggy!"

"Go fall off a bridge!" I yelled after them, and they waved. One of them turned out to be in my class at school, and she really wasn't a bad kid. Kids in the country just don't know much—they hardly get out of their own backyards, except to ride to town in the car.

In New York all you've got to do is walk around the block and you see a lot of things, like guys trying to hoist a piano up the side of a tall building to get it in a window, or two old men arguing with each other because one of them didn't pay the other his rent. It's interesting.

Of course in the country there's worms and frogs and trees to climb. After we got home and I revived with a bowl of cereal, I went out to sit in the treehouse.

Pigtails was standing in her yard. She climbed up and stood on one foot on top of a fence post, so she could look down on me. I'm not much good at climbing and balancing on top of things.

"We bought Cokes and Zooms at the store," I said.

"Whoever heard of Zooms?" she said.

"It's a new kind of cereal and they give you a free rocket launcher in every package, but it doesn't work very well."

"Those are baby toys," she sniffed. "Anyway, what's your name?"

"Berries . . . Goodman."

"Berries! Huh! Berries is for the birds! Is that *really* your name?"

"It's a nickname, stupid. What's yours?"

"I don't have a nickname." She looked momentarily sad about it. "My name is Sandra Graham."

"They could call you Sandy."

"They don't, though. How old are you?"

"Nine."

"I'm almost eleven. You have to be eleven to be in the Pony Club and ride cross-country." Having established her superiority, Sandra jumped off the fence post and suggested climbing into the treehouse.

I said, "O.K. It's in pretty bad shape, now—needs a lot of repairs. I'm going to put on a new roof and get a lot of furniture."

"Hey, we can make it our clubhouse!" she said. I didn't quite realize at first that she had invited herself to the club with that "we" stuff, but she moved right on to elect herself boss.

"We got to make some rules for the club. Dues, ten cents . . . uh, how much allowance do you get?"

"Fifty cents a week."

"You're lying. Nobody nine gets that much."

"I do too! I did in New York anyway. I had to pay Cub Scouts, and buy skate keys and balls and save for a baseball mitt, and I hardly ever even had enough left for ice cream."

"It still isn't fair. I only get twenty-five. We'll make dues five cents."

"Who gets the dues?"

"The club, stupid. I'll be treasurer. We got to buy supplies—food and stuff—and get ammunition for the war chest. We have to have rules, too: nobody allowed in the club under nine years old, no tattletales, no finks—"

"Huh?"

"You know, teacher's pets, anyone you don't like. My sister calls everyone finks. Now, we can have try-outs. Everyone has to chin themselves five times and do three cartwheels."

Sandra swung out and gripped one of the branches under the treehouse and chinned herself. She dropped to the ground and did cartwheels all around the tree.

"Now you," she said.

I managed to chin myself all right. Then I dropped down, dusted off my hands, and said, "I don't feel like cartwheels right now. Besides, it's more important to have some kind of a test for throwing things at the enemy. Everyone stand by the house and see if they can hit the tree with a baseball four throws out of five."

34

I threw and hit the tree three times, and Sandra couldn't hit it at all. She said, "That's a crumby test. You couldn't even do it yourself."

"Gimme the ball. I bet—"

"Oh, I don't know that I even *want* to start a club," she said.

"So don't! It happens to be *my* treehouse, and I might have a club for boys only."

"Yeah, baby boys!"

"Sissy!"

She went home, and I stood and threw stones from the driveway at the tree. I hit it five times in a row.

Dad came home and told me stones on the lawn were bad for the the lawnmower, which Hal later found to be true.

"Our neighbors," I told Dad, "have got a girl."

"Good. So've we."

"Not a baby—a girl! Here we are, miles from nowhere, with no food and no candy bars, and I get nothing but one lousy girl for a neighbor! She goes horseback riding and she can walk on her hands."

"That's what really hurts, isn't it?" said Hal.

"Why don't you mind your own business?"

Dad said, "We must have other neighbors too, so don't worry. I'm sure there are boys your age nearby—they'll come to fish in the pond. The important question is, what's for dinner?"

"There wouldn't even *be* any dinner if Hal and I hadn't walked miles to town pushing the baby buggy to get it! We were starving, and I about died of thirst on the way home."

Dad said, "I warned you—pioneering is tough."

4

Neighbors

Dad was wrong about there being plenty of boys nearby. That first summer I had to make do with Sandra, and life with her followed a pretty regular pattern. We'd get together and think of a project, and she'd insist on being the chief and me being the loyal slob. After a while we'd get into a fight and one of us would go home in a huff.

The huffs never lasted very long, though. I didn't have any other friends to fall back on. Sandra put up with me because she liked to show off, and she really could do almost everything better than me, even boys' things like jumping and climbing and taking dares. Her muscles all seemed to work right, so she hardly ever had to be scared. I was hefty and my feet kept getting tangled up, and people would yell at me for knocking things over. I didn't knock them. They just fell when I went by.

Another thing was, Sandra had a lot of problems with her family. Her sister was seventeen and stuck-up. She always called us "you brats." I hardly ever saw Sandra's father, but he had this pedigreed Irish setter named Patrick, and Sandra said she bet he loved Patrick more than he did her. I don't suppose he did, but they wouldn't let Sandra have a dog of her own because Patrick was already there, and he was a thoroughbred and special. He was a dumb dog—he wouldn't play or anything.

But the worst was Sandra's mother. For the first week or so I just *heard* her: a trumpeting call from the Grahams' back door, "San-DRA!" There was nothing friendly about that call; it never sounded as if she'd *like* to see Sandra. Sandra always went right away, not ten minutes later, the way I do when Mom calls.

Mrs. Graham had a rule about everything. One rule was that Sandra wasn't allowed to play indoors unless it was raining or dark out. So Sandra was pretty glad to have a kid next door, even if it was only me.

I didn't meet her mother officially until about the second rainy day. We were up in Sandra's room playing Monopoly, perfectly quiet, not making any mess. Her mother had been out, but she came back and came up to Sandra's room. She cleared her throat: "San-*dra!*" It wasn't quite as loud as the backyard call, but the same tone of voice.

We were sitting on the floor, and she looked awfully tall. Even after I got to know her better, I never thought of her as anything but big and hard like a bulldozer. She was never either pretty or sloppy.

"Oh, hello, Mom—it was raining, so we came in," Sandra explained.

"*San*-dra." Obviously, she was prompting.

Sandra scrambled up. "Mother, this is Berries Goodman. They just moved in next door."

"How do you do—ah, did you say Berries?"

"That's right. My real name's Bertrand, but nobody calls me that."

"Mmm." Mrs. Graham looked as if she disapproved of Bertrand and Berries about equally. "Sandra, another time, show your little friend where to put his wet things, so he doesn't have to leave them dripping in the front hall."

This seemed to be a crack at me as much as at Sandra, and anyway I didn't like that "little friend" business. Mrs. Graham went downstairs, and I looked at Sandra with a certain amount of sympathy. She just sat down and said, "It's my play."

It wasn't, either. She quite often cheated. I let her get away with it that time, because I was winning.

Monopoly is rather a long dull game. I was practically sure to win, when Sandra looked out the window and said, "It's almost stopped raining. We better go out."

"You really get pushed around, don't you?" I said.

"*My* mother is very strict, that's all," Sandra said. The funny thing is, she acted as if she was proud of it.

All of this might sound as if Sandra was a pain in the neck, but really she was pretty good fun to play with. She liked to catch frogs and salamanders down at the pond, and she was always ready to bat or throw a ball with me—it was one of the few things I could do as well as she could. She did learn to hit the tree four throws out of five quite soon, and I never did learn to walk on my hands. I guess when two kids live next door and see each other most every day, they just get used to each other's faults and they feel like friends.

Sandra knew her way around town much better than I did, and one day she took me exploring and fishing down the George River. The trouble with that expedition was, we started too late, and it was evening when Hal picked us up in the car, miles from home.

"Boy, are you going to get it from Mom!" Some welcome.

Mom has never seen any sense in fishing unless you bring home fish. She doesn't approve of exploring at all. I'd intended to drift home as if I'd just been at

Sandra's, so as soon as I saw Hal out as a search party I knew I was in trouble.

Hal told Mom where he'd found us, and before I could stop her, Sandra explained that we'd been fishing in the George. Mom hit the roof.

"Down where all those cliffs are! Besides, there are probably gangs of hoodlums living in those woods!"

"It's perfectly safe," Sandra said. "We didn't see anyone, and we go around the cliffs."

Mom slapped her forehead. "Uh-h! Come along, I want to talk to your mother."

Mom is funny about other kids' mothers. I think she's afraid of them, so I knew she had to be pretty worked up to call on Mrs. Graham.

She knocked on the front door, and Mrs. Graham came and said, "Good evening! Goodness, I hope Sandra hasn't been in your house all this time." She made it sound as if it had been Mom's fault to allow it.

"She certainly has not! I hate to complain, but I think you really ought to know that these children were playing on the cliffs down on the river. I won't allow Berries off the place again."

In a sugary voice Mrs. Graham said, "I'm sorry you were worried. Of course, Sandra mustn't take your little boy so far. She has been fishing down there before, and we want her to be self-reliant."

41

Mom looked ready to explode, but she swallowed hard and just said, "Good night."

"Thank you for coming," said Mrs. Graham, obviously not meaning it.

When we were back in our own yard, Mom said, "Self-reliant—hogwash! You can just be self-reliant about getting home for supper on time and not leaving our yard again without permission. See?"

It didn't seem like a good time to argue.

I found out the next day that Mrs. Graham sent Sandra up to her room without supper, as soon as we'd left. The big cheese—she just wouldn't let on that anyone but Mrs. Graham could be right! I suppose she thought us Goodmans didn't count because we didn't go to the Country Club and the Pony Club, and she was always telling me "Run home and put on a clean shirt, dear" before she'd even let me ride to the store with them.

She bossed Mr. Graham too, Sandra said, but when he wasn't working, he was mostly out hunting or improving the grounds around the house. Sandra said they were going to sell their house for a lot of money and buy a better one. Sandra always talked big. She liked to tell me all their plans and all these complicated rules her mother made up. I think she had to act proud of the rules because her mother never did any little nice things for her, like giving her a kiss or buying her a little present for no reason.

Sandra sure liked coming into our house to be comfortable, though, and we played with all my stuff till I was sick of it. Actually, Sandra had lots better toys than I did, and even a ping-pong table in the cellar. The first few times Sandra was at our house, I was trying to show off what we had.

I opened the icebox door and said, "Gee, no Cokes!" as if I was really surprised.

Helpful Hal said, "What do you think this is, a holiday?"

"I don't like Coke anyway," said Sandra.

"You do too; you're faking. I know, you pretend you don't like television too, just because you're not allowed to watch in the evening."

Sandra sniffed. "I do not either like Coke. It makes me feel sick. Besides, Mom says it rots your teeth."

She was heaping sugar into chocolate milk at the moment, and Hal said, "I suppose you think all that sugar doesn't rot your teeth, too!"

Sandra turned up her nose. "Of course not. Milk's good for your teeth; it's full of calcium. Anybody knows that. I guess you're not in the accelerated section of your class, I just guess you're not!"

"Aw, you can have an accelerated kick in the

pants!" Sandra spilled some of her milk, and Hal skated out the door, saying, "Serves you right!"

"Teenagers! They think they're so great!" said Sandra.

"My friend Irvy in New York, he's always in an accelerated class," I said. "He's really bright."

Sandra puckered up her mouth. "Irvy. I never heard of anyone named Irvy."

"Well, his name is Irvy Weinstein, and he's my best friend."

"Oh—Weinstein. That's Jewish."

"So what? His father's rich; he owns a whole bakery and he brings home fresh bagels and cakes and stuff every day."

"Jews are all rich. My Dad says they get all the money."

"Why shouldn't Irvy's father get the money, anyway? It's his bakery."

"You're just too little to understand," Sandra sniffed.

"I just wish Irvy was out here. He's still my best friend."

"Did he live right near you?"

"Course he did. He lived right next door and sat behind me in school."

"Out *here*," said Sandra, "the Jews all live out around Indian Road and the Acres. They have this fancy club, with doormen in shiny uniforms, and pink plush carpets in the bathrooms, and they all drive up in—"

Hal had come back and was standing in the doorway listening to Sandra. He said, "You practicing to be some kind of a Nazi or something?"

"Nazi? Who's a . . ." Sandra floundered. "Stupid, Nazis are Germans and we beat them in the war."

"Well, you sound just like one. Don't you know the Nazis rounded up the Jewish people and put them in one part of town, and then they put them in concentration camps, and then they killed millions of them?"

Sandra stuck her lip out. "I didn't say anything about *killing* anyone."

"You sound like Jewish people shouldn't live next door to you."

"Course not. Mom says they'd grab all the best real estate and build these big showy houses and—"

"There you go again, Nazi! For your information, the Jews I know are a whole lot nicer than you. And they don't make as much noise."

"Yeah, you just wait," I put in. "*My* friend Irvy's father might come and buy your house, and then they'd be our neighbors. He could do it, too."

"He could not! Jewish people can't buy a house on this street. My Mom says."

"You're really off your rocker," Hal said. "Anyone

can buy a house if it's for sale."

"And your father wants to sell yours. I hope I get some decent neighbors then," I said.

"Well, I guess I have plenty of other friends. I don't have to stay here and argue with you! I hope we do move!"

"Hurry up about it!" I said. Sandra flounced out the door, and that was the end of another day.

I pretty nearly always made up with Sandra the next day. Since the fishing expedition, I gathered Mom wasn't too fond of Mrs. Graham, and I pretty much stayed out of their house and steered clear of her. I don't mind if my own mother yells at me, but I don't like to take chances on anyone else's.

There was one muggy afternoon when we'd run out of things to do, and we were in Sandra's yard trying to hitch Patrick up to pull the express wagon. He kept lying down.

"When I get my dog, I'm going to train him to pull a cart," I said.

Mrs. Graham came out on their porch with her sewing, and she told Sandra to let Patrick go. She said to me quite pleasantly, "You must be going to get an Eskimo Husky then, is that right?"

"Uh, well, Dad said I could get a dog in the country and Mom said we might go to the dog pound and find one that's small and quiet and doesn't shed too much. But we didn't go yet."

"I see, not a thoroughbred," said Mrs. Graham, as if that meant it would hardly be a dog at all. "You should go to the Humane Society. They sometimes have nice puppies for children."

"Mom works for the Society. She's vice-president," said Sandra.

"The next time I'm down, I'll ask if they have a good litter," said Mrs. Graham.

"Mom," said Sandra, squatting beside her mother and speaking very politely, "please, Mom, couldn't I get one too? We could train them together. I'd take really good care of him, honest I would."

"One dog is enough, dear, and we have Patrick. Besides, Daddy said he'd get you a pony as soon as you can ride well enough to train one. That'll take up all your time."

"It might be *years* before he gets the pony!"

"You must keep working, dear."

"Work!" Sandra dug her heel savagely into the lawn. "That's just an excuse, anyway. I bet if I was a boy, Daddy would get me a puppy."

"What a silly thing to say, Sandra. Don't make holes in the lawn."

"It's not silly. If I was a boy, Daddy'd get me lots of things, and he'd take me with him hunting, too. He even *says* so—he says he has to go hunting to get away from all us women."

"Sandra, you're talking nonsense. You'd better go up to your room. Lots of boys don't have puppies, and you have so many other things already, you should be grateful."

The screen door slammed behind Sandra, and she shouted through it: "Grateful, hateful!"

Mrs. Graham pursed her lips and said, "Good night, Berries; we'll see you another day."

I guessed I'd better depend on my own parents to find a puppy, because I didn't want to ask Mrs. Graham and get Sandra all stirred up again. Mom kept saying Dad would go with me Saturday, and Dad always said he had too much work to do on the house. A run-around, that's what.

Late in August the phone rang one day. Mom spoke in her puckery, extra polite tone of voice. "It's so so kind of you to bother . . . no, I didn't know he'd asked you. . . . Of course he'd like to look at them. I'll have his father take him Saturday. . . . Thank you, of course we'll let you know."

Mom put the phone down and turned to glare at me. "Did you ask Mrs. Graham to find you a puppy?"

"I never did! I was just talking, and I said maybe I'd get one, and she said—"

"Well, she's taken it upon herself to locate a litter

48

for you to look at. Part beagle she said they were, and way down in Oxford. Daddy'll have a fit."

"Beagles are very cute. They're small, you know, and they have smooth coats that don't shed." Luckily, this all turned out to be true.

"Well, Daddy'll have to take you Saturday. He can decide," Mom said.

"Yippee!" I blasted off the kitchen stool and out the door. Behind me I heard the sound of things falling. Ordinarily, I would have run on but I thought, Poor Mom, she's always picking up after Jennifer; I better not make her mad right now. I went back and picked up the stool and swept the spilled cereal off the floor. Mom stared. I went up in the treehouse and started trying out names for a dog. "Here, Bullet! Here, Jock! Spooky. Mickey. Here, Mickey, boy!" They all sounded good.

Dad took me that weekend. There were half a dozen puppies in this cage they showed us, all yelping and climbing on each other. I reached my hand in, and a white one with a brown patch over one eye climbed right into my hand. The brown patch made him look spooky, as if he were winking.

"Hey, Spook! Hello, Spooky, boy!" He scrambled up to my chest and made darting licks at my mouth.

The man was talking. "The two mostly white ones are the females. The others are males."

"You mean this one is a girl?"

49

"That's right."

I looked at the pup again, considering. I'd never thought of having a girl dog. The pup clambered up my jacket and nipped my ear. I looked down at all the others wriggling and yapping. The one that had chosen me was really the cutest.

"This one's gotten to know me," I said. "I'll keep him—her, I mean."

The attendant looked at Dad. Dad frowned and shrugged. "I guess it's all right. But if she has puppies, your mother will have kittens."

"Puppies! That's great! I can give one to Sandra."

"Stop giving away puppies before they're hatched. We don't *want* puppies."

We got in the car, and Spook made a puddle in the front seat right away. Dad groaned. "This is just the beginning. Puddles. Messes. Chewed-up books and shoes. Why'd we get into this?"

Mom made me call Mrs. Graham to thank her and tell her about the pup. I thought Sandra would be down any minute, but she wasn't. She didn't come the next morning either—she always went to Sunday school—and it wasn't till afternoon, when I was out in the yard with Spook, that I saw her leaning over the fence.

"Is that him?" she said dully.

"It's her. Her name is Spook."

Sandra climbed over the fence. She put her hand out and Spooky licked it.

"You can pick her up," I said, but she didn't. We didn't say anything for a minute. I guessed she felt pretty bad about not having a puppy herself.

"Did you go to the Pony Club?" I asked.

"Uh-huh. We went on a real cross-country ride for two hours, and we cantered a lot. My father better get me my horse soon."

"Does he go riding with you?"

Sandra's face closed again. "He's too busy. Every day he works, and Saturday he takes Patrick pheasant shooting. Sunday morning I have to go to Sunday school. There's never any time."

"What about Sunday afternoon?"

"He's tired." Sandra sat, with her chin on her fists, looking gloomily at Spook. She looked away over the pond, and her face got dreamy.

"Once last year, when I was getting over chicken pox, I didn't go to Sunday school. Daddy played ball with me, and then we went for a walk with Patrick. We walked for hours."

Sandra talked as if this was the greatest thing that had ever happened.

Spooky saw a flying moth and started after it. She jumped over Sandra's foot, but Sandra picked her foot up and tripped her. She did it on purpose, I know—she had a mean look on her face.

I grabbed her by the pigtail and yanked. "You did that on purpose! You just better leave my dog alone!"

She pulled away from me, and I was surprised to see she was crying. She yelled, "I don't care, I hate your old dog!"

I picked up Spooky, who wasn't hurt, and went indoors. That was about the only time I saw Sandra cry.

5

Friend

I was looking forward to Labor Day so school would begin. It's not that I liked school all that much, but I wanted to get to know some other kids. Mom just doesn't call people up to ask if their little boy can come over to play. Dad took me to the village recreation field to swim a few times, but all the other kids already knew each other, and I didn't really get into the gang. Anyway, I didn't go very often—Dad would say I could swim in our own pond. Grown-ups are dopey about some things.

Sandra said the school bus came at seven twenty in the morning, and she was right. As soon as we got on it the first day, she went to sit with a bunch of cackling girls. There were some boys about my age in the back of the bus, shouting and punching each other. I stood by the driver, and when we stopped he showed me how the automatic blinking stop light worked.

I got assigned a seat in the front row in my classroom, and I could hear all the kids behind me whispering. I'd catch bits like "He's new," so I felt as if all the whispering was about me. The teacher handed us paper to write our names and a paragraph about what we'd done that summer. My writing was sort of messy. When I was finished, the girl next to me looked at my paper and whispered to her neighbor, "He's printing!"

On the other side of me a rather fat boy wrote, "Julie is a big pig" on a bit of paper and pushed it to me, and pointed to the little girl. His writing was worse than my printing, so I felt better, and I didn't pay any more attention to Julie.

They really had recess at this school—I mean you went outdoors and played. In the city we just had milk and crackers, and you could talk to your neighbor, or else we played Simon Says. The girls all hogged the swings at the beginning of recess, and the boys divided into two volleyball teams. I went and balanced on a seesaw. There was a girl sitting on the high swinging bar, just sitting there and talking, not swinging, and this slim, dark-haired boy came and told her he wanted to swing.

"I got here first," she said and poked her foot in his

face. He grabbed it and swung her back and forth, and she squealed and finally jumped down. Like a flock of starlings, the other girls all decided to leave the swings and swarm over the jungle gym. I grabbed a swing, and this kid grabbed the high bar and soon was hanging by his knees, swinging almost as hard as I was.

"Gee, you're pretty good at that," I said.

"Yeah," he said. He didn't sound stuck-up, and I was glad he didn't say "It's easy," because I knew I couldn't do it.

He pulled himself right side up and said, "Where'd you live before you came here?"

"In New York—in the city."

"I went in last spring with my older brother. We went up the Empire State and to a movie at Radio City and everything."

"I didn't go up the Empire State yet," I said.

He looked amazed. "Gee, and you lived right *there!* I'd go all the time—"

The recess bell rang and we walked in together and he said, "See you," as he went off to his seat in the back row. We had arithmetic after recess, which takes me a long time, and I didn't get all the examples for homework copied down. Neither did the kid next to me. "Homework, the first day," he grumbled. "It's no fair."

I hoped the kid from the swing would give me the homework, but I didn't want to ask him at lunch. He was sitting next to the teacher. In the afternoon we went out for play period, and I got next to him in the ring organized for dodgeball. On about the third row he hit the kid, and then it was his turn in the middle. All the other kids groaned, "It takes too long to get Sidney out! We'll never get a turn." It did take a long time, too—he was very fast. Toward the end I got a turn, and I knew I'd probably be out about the first throw. Sidney had the ball, and he threw it too high. Somehow, I knew he missed me on purpose. The next kid got me.

I asked him if I could copy the homework while we were on the bus. "Sure," he said, and opened his notebook. He had the answers down under all the examples.

"Gee, you've done them already!"

"Sure, I always do them while I'm copying them, as long as they're easy."

"Doesn't look easy to me," I said.

"You'll probably catch on, after you get used to the school and everything."

"Yeah . . ." I started doubtfully, but then the bus was at my stop and Sandra was already standing by the door. I jumped up. "S'long!"

" 'Bye." Sidney nodded his head, and then he fished another book out of his schoolbag and settled down to read it. He didn't take much part in all the bouncing and yelling the other kids did on the bus.

The first couple of school days seemed long, long,

and I was always kind of sneaking looks out of the corner of my eye to explore something new. Then suddenly it was Friday, and I could hardly remember how I could have felt so new. Everything looked familiar, as if I'd been there a long time. There were only about twenty kids in our class, and I knew their names and which ones were best friends.

Sidney didn't seem to have a best friend. At recess he joined the ball games sometimes, and he was always one of the best players, but he wasn't ever the captain, because he wasn't noisy or bossy enough. He didn't care a lot about games anyway, and some recesses he went off by himself to swing on the bar or walk on his hands. I thought, I bet he could beat old Sandra; she's always showing off the tricks she can do.

There were two or three other boys I got to know pretty fast, but they each had a best friend or two that they stuck with, and I didn't want to be a tag-along. I got in the habit of teaming up with Sidney, on the bus or in the playground. I liked him for a funny reason—I mean funny for a kid: He was very polite. Usually you don't like a kid who makes a big deal out of *please* and *thank you*, and plays up to the grown-ups all the time. But Sidney was really polite—like if I made a goof in some game, he tried to cover it up, and when I asked him to explain some arithmetic, he just explained. Most kids have to show off how bright they are and how dopey you are even to ask that question.

We'd been in school a couple of weeks when Sidney came up one recess and said, "My mom's coming to pick me up at school today. Can you come home with me? I got to go get a haircut first, but that won't take long."

"Uh, gee, that'd be great. But I don't know about my mom."

"We can phone her. I'll get Mom to phone her as soon as she comes."

"O.K."

Along about the middle of the afternoon I thought, Supposing Mom says No, and then I've already missed the school bus. . . .

But it didn't turn out that way. Mom was sort of startled, and then she was worried she'd have to come get me, and she hates driving with Jennifer. Mrs. Fine said of course she'd bring me home, so that was all right.

We got Sidney's hair cut and drove to his house. It was the end house of all those neat new ones with white fences that Miss Real Estate had shown us the first day we came to Olcott. Sidney's house was older than the others, and a little bigger. We went inside, and Mrs. Fine asked if I wanted grape juice or Coke or something else. I gulped and said, "Grape juice, please." She put a plate of brownies on the table and a plate of bagels too, and I had one of each. Sidney took three brownies, and his mother didn't stop him. She took one herself and said she shouldn't, and then she had another.

Mrs. Fine treated us an awful lot like grown-ups. She asked did we want to do this or that, and what was my favorite TV program, and where did my father work, and did Hal know Sidney's older brother, Marty. She also got angry with Sidney if he did something childish, like sputtering and laughing so that he spilled his drink. She asked him what marks he got on all his papers, and she knew exactly where we were in school on each subject. My mom doesn't even know what book I'm on, hardly. I guess it'd be nice to have your mother know all about your schoolwork. Except then you'd have to work harder, the way Sidney did.

He changed his clothes—I wear blue jeans to school, so it doesn't matter—and we went out to play. There were plenty of kids in Sidney's neighborhood, and they all seemed pretty nice. Somebody lent me a bike, and then another kid let me use his football helmet. When it was getting dark, Mrs. Fine called us in to supper, and she gave Sidney a hug and me a pat on the head, just as if she hadn't seen us for a real long time. When people pat you on the head as if you were a cute little dog, it makes you sore, but this was just a nice sort of welcome. Also, she had a real pizza pie for supper, and that's always welcome.

Between bites, I said, "Gee, you cook awfully good food!"

Mrs. Fine laughed and said she bet my mother was a good cook too, and I couldn't exactly say anything. Mrs. Fine went upstairs, and Sidney and I got to talking.

"Your mom is nice," I said. "She doesn't treat us like dopey little kids, the way lots of mothers do."

"She won't *let* me be a dopey little kid," said Sidney, biting off a long string of pizza cheese. "She always wants me to be perfect, and boy, does she get upset sometimes!"

"What about?"

"Well, it's especially if I get hurt. She picked me up at school that day I got a scratch down my cheek in a volleyball game, and she dragged me into the principal's office to find out all about it. She was sure someone did it on purpose. There's other things, too. Yesterday I broke a plate my grandmother gave us, and you'd think the house had fallen in."

"Oh, well, grown-ups are always flying off about something," I said. "I still think you're pretty lucky. We *never* have a real pizza pie at home. Besides, you've got all the kids around here to play with. I've just got Sandra."

"There are always plenty of kids in a development," Sidney said.

"What's a development?"

"This is. Olcott Acres. My father built it."

"Gosh, he must be rich. We haven't got enough money to buy even *one* house."

"He's not specially rich," said Sidney. "He owned this land for a long time, and he gets banks or something to lend him the money to build houses and then he sells them."

I found out later that Sidney's father was not especially rich. He'd been sick and he sold the newspaper store he used to run in the village, and the development was sort of his business now. I also found out it's quite hard to tell who is rich, anyway. People who have big cars and their kids have shiny bicycles sometimes aren't really rich at all.

Mrs. Fine came downstairs and got ready to take me home. I remembered to thank her for dinner and everything. I didn't usually remember this, but somehow around Mrs. Fine it seemed natural. I really was glad she'd asked me. "See you Monday," I said to Sidney.

"Not till Tuesday," he said. "It's Rosh Hashanah."

"Yippee! You mean we get a three-day holiday?"

"It's not a school holiday," Mrs. Fine said.

Sidney said, "I just get to stay home because we have a big family party."

"Gee, in New York it was a holiday for everyone. What a gyp!" I said.

When I got home, I asked Mom how come it wasn't a holiday for everyone out here.

"I guess there just aren't so many Jewish families out here," she said. "Why don't you look in school Monday and see how many kids are absent?"

So I did, and there was only one—Sidney.

I went to Sidney's house several times, and then one day at school he said, "When are you going to invite me to your house?"

I scratched my head. "I'll have to ask Mom. I've never really asked anyone to my house. Except Sandra, and she just comes."

"Who's she?"

"You know, she's in sixth grade and has pigtails and is captain of the girls' volleyball. She lives next to us."

Sidney made a face. "So when are you going to ask your mother?"

"Uh, I'll ask her tonight."

I wanted Sidney to come all right, but I wasn't too anxious to ask Mom. She's funny about things like that. She'd gotten used to Sandra, who just wandered in and out. Also, Mom talks by the hour on the telephone to old friends of her own, but she sure hates to get on the phone to people she doesn't know and arrange about invitations.

"Is it all right if I bring Sidney home with me to-morrow?" I asked at dinner. "You don't have to call them up; I'll just bring him on the bus."

Mom looked faintly alarmed, but she said all right. Sidney came the next day, and after we'd had some chocolate milk, and cereal because we were out of cookies, Sidney started up the steps, figuring to go up to my room. He looked in and saw it was Mom's dead-end bathroom.

"That's neat!" he said. "It's a hideaway!"

Mom looked pleased. "That's the way I feel about it too," she said.

We went outside and over to the treehouse. I climbed up by some steps I'd nailed to the tree trunk, but Sidney ran and jumped and caught the branch to swing himself up, like Tarzan. He was shorter than me, but he could do it easily. I showed him the book of secret codes, and we added a new one that he knew.

I heard a whistle down below and Sandra's voice: "Hey, Berries!"

"Yeah?"

"Whatcha doing?"

"Playing with Sidney."

Pause. "Who's he?"

Sidney stuck his head out to look down, and I said, "Sidney Fine. He's in my class."

"Oh, him," Sandra said.

"Oh, her," said Sidney.

"I never said he could be in the club," said Sandra.

"Well, it happens to be my treehouse, smarty, and he happens to be my friend."

"You're a traitor to the club."

"Let's pour boiling oil on the attacker!" said Sidney. He picked up handfuls of leaves and pine needles and threw them down. Sandra had to shut her eyes and back away, and we both laughed and threw some more. She stamped away.

"I'm glad I've got someone besides a *girl* to play with," I said, and Sidney looked pleased. I was sick of being Sandra's loyal slob.

It was some kind of half holiday that day, and Dad came home early. He came out under the treehouse to rake leaves, and I introduced him to Sidney.

"Hi, Sidney," Dad said. "Berries is sure glad to find a real live boy around here."

"This is a neat treehouse you have. I wish I had one. I like your big house, too—especially the bathroom hideaway."

Dad laughed. "That's where Berries' mother goes to get away from us all when she feels grumpy."

Sidney said, "When *my* mother's cross, *I* go and hide!"

"Well, I guess it works out either way," said Dad.

64

I looked up and saw Sandra's father coming down toward us, and Sandra behind him. Mr. Graham was sort of big and red-faced, and he made a lot of jokes in a loud voice. With Sandra's mother, you knew where you stood—you were just about always wrong. With Sandra's father, you couldn't tell. Sometimes when he came home at night, he was very jolly and brought Sandra some little present, but other nights he snapped at her for no reason. If we made too much noise in the morning on weekends, he got really cross.

He and Sandra both had paint cans and brushes and scrapers, and they came down to paint the fence that separates our property. Sandra made sure we could see she was eating a big frosted cookie.

"Daddy bought me this in New York," she said.

Sidney sniffed. "My mother makes cookies almost every day. She doesn't like store cookies."

Mr. Graham was chatting with Dad. "Always something to do around a house, isn't there? This old paint is murder to scrape."

Dad was leaning on his rake, which he does a good deal. He said, "I want to get a good compost pile of leaves to use on the garden next year."

Mr. Graham was scraping paint busily. He shouted, "Used to grow a garden myself. Gave it up though—took too much time. I've got all I can do to keep the house and yard in shape."

He straightened up for a minute, and it seemed to me that he cast a look toward our house, with its peeling paint and yard littered with old toys.

Dad made a few cheerful swipes with the rake. "Well, I guess it's lucky I'm not a homeowner. I'm no good at that do-it-yourself stuff."

"I *had* to get good at it," Mr. Graham said. "Adelaide can't stand things looking run-down; she's always after me. Besides, we hope to sell this house in a few years. With the improvements I've put in and everything in good shape, I ought to get almost double what I paid for it. This neighborhood is changing. Those new houses down the road—people throwing money around. No taste. Adelaide wants to move over near the Country Club."

"Well, goodness knows where we'll be in a few years," said Dad. He didn't sound worried about it, and Mr. Graham gave a short bark of a laugh, not as if anything was funny.

Sidney's mother drove up our road then, and Sidney shouted to her to come look at the treehouse.

She came over and said, "Goodness, boys, be careful you don't fall!"

Sandra had to get into the act, of course. She swung up onto a branch and hung by her knees, making it look as dangerous as possible. Mrs. Fine gasped and looked at Dad.

"They're just trying to scare you. They've really never hurt themselves," he said. "I'm Berries' father, Dan Goodman. I'm afraid Berries didn't tell me your last name."

"Fine, Miriam Fine," she said, and they shook hands and both watched us doing tricks in the tree for a bit. Sandra's father finished a section of fence and stood up. Dad said, "This is Mrs. Fine. My neighbor, Mac-Arthur Graham."

"How do you do? My, you have a lovely house there," said Mrs. Fine.

"How do." He just barely nodded, and then he barked at Sandra: "Quit showing off in that tree, Sandra. Go and ask Mother if supper is ready."

"Aw, gee, it's not that late . . ." Sandra started. Then she saw the look he gave her, and she jumped down and started home. He went back to painting.

"Come along, Sidney, it's late. You're keeping everyone waiting," said Mrs. Fine. Suddenly her voice was abrupt too. Grown-ups are hard to tell about. One minute they're chatting, and then all of a sudden a chill sets in.

"Gee, why'd you have to come so early?" Sidney said.

Mrs. Fine said, "Come *on!*"

"You come again real soon, Sidney," said Dad, trying to smooth things over.

Sidney and his mother walked to their car. I waved and shouted, "See you tomorrow," and he waved back. I was sorry they left that way. It was the first time Sidney had been to my house, and I wanted him to like everything.

Sandra came knocking at the door on the weekend.

"Whatcha doing?"

"Nothing much. Has it stopped raining?"

"Yes, but they cancelled the Pony Club ride. I was going to go for two hours. It's a gyp."

"I'm going to Hal's school to watch the football game this afternoon."

"Can I come?"

"Umm, I don't know. Girls don't play football."

"Well, I can *watch!* I know all the rules; you'll see." That was the trouble with Sandra—she knew all about everything.

"Let's go out in the treehouse and see if the roof leaked," I said.

We went and patched the roof a little, and Sandra looked in the code book at the new code Sidney had added. She said, "Huh, anyone knows that baby code!"

I didn't say anything, because this was often the best way to answer Sandra.

"How come you had to pick *him* for a friend?" she said.

"I like him. You ought to see him walk on his hands. I bet you can't."

"Neither can you. Anyhow, don't you know he's the only Jew in Olcott Corners school? So why'd you have to pick *him?*"

"I told you, I like him. So what if he's Jewish? They get Rosh Hashanah off. I wish I did."

"They get *what?*"

"Gee, don't you even know what Rosh Hashanah is? You must be stupid or something. It's the Jewish New Year's Day."

"I don't even *want* to know. Anyway, he's not even meant to be in our school. He just sneaked in. I heard Mom say."

"That's dumb. Anyone can go to a public school."

"No one else from Olcott Acres goes to our school. He sneaked in."

"He did not."

"He did so!"

"I'm going to find Hal and see if it's time for the football game." I knew that'd get her, so I jumped down from the tree and strolled toward the house.

Before I reached the back door, she was beside me.

69

"O.K., I take it back. He didn't sneak in. Do you think Hal would mind if I come?"

"I guess he can stand it," I said, like a big shot.

6

Mother's Outing

Along in December, I noticed that Mom had been really grouchy for several days, and I realized that she was sort of bogged down in the country. I mean literally bogged down: There was practically no one there to talk to from sunrise to sunset except Jennifer, who yowled.

My school bus got me home at four. Hal usually didn't come till later, because he was on so many clubs and teams. It was almost eight before Dad arrived—he didn't hurry much now that there was no gardening or picnicking to look forward to. Finally Mom made Hal resign from orchestra so he could come home early Wednesdays, and she could have her weekly outing at the A & P.

"Outing!" Dad snorted. "I don't call the A & P an outing. What do the other mothers do for fun?"

"Probably they play bridge." Mom made a face, because she doesn't. "I don't know—I never *have* known what other mothers do. Besides, I hardly see any, except at the store. *They* don't have an outing, though. They take their little monsters with them, all sticky and runny-nosed and shrieking for bubble gum. Ghastly!"

"They keep them in pens when they're home, though," said Hal.

"So the mothers have time to make brownies and stuff," I added. "Listen, why don't we fence in a yard for Jennifer *and* Spooky? And they'd keep each other happy and there wouldn't be so many messes in the house."

Dad bought some snow fence and we built a yard. The trouble was, Spook made messes in it, and then it wasn't so good for Jennifer. By the middle of winter it seemed to me Jennifer had a cold all the time anyway, so Mom always had her indoors, dripping and whining. Jennifer didn't like to play with things like trucks and blocks or even dolls: She wanted people to play games with her. Since she hardly spoke English anyway, it was very frustrating. For her and Mom, I mean. The rest of us got out.

I came home one Wednesday and found Mom arguing with Hal, which is rather unusual.

"There'll be basketball games on Saturdays," Hal protested. "I'm on the holiday dance committee too. And what about my homework?"

"Daddy and Berries can manage while you go to basketball. Let someone else do the dance; it's not that important—"

"Not important! It's only the biggest dance of the year!"

"—and you can do your homework in the evenings."

"Gee, thanks." Hal scowled and thought a minute and then started on a new tack. "What about Dad? You'll never see him. Pretty soon you'll be talking about divorce. Lots of kids' parents get divorces because their mothers work."

"They do not," said Mom. "Besides, Daddy is perfectly happy all weekend stamping around in the snow or sawing wood, or whatever it is that he does out there. In summer he'll have the garden."

Hal groaned and I finally got a word in. "What *is* all this?"

Mom waved the local paper, the Oxford one, opened to the want ad page. "There's an ad for an assistant salesman in a real estate office. Selling houses. I just realized it—selling houses is what I've always wanted to do. I like to look at them and think about them. I never really wanted to buy one."

"How can *you* be a salesman?"

"Silly, it doesn't matter whether you're a man or a lady. I'd be like Miss Real Estate."

"I don't see why you want to be like *that!*" I said. "Who's going to cook dinner and look after things around here?"

"You and your stomach! To begin with, I'd only work Saturdays and Sundays, and you can eat hot dogs and bologna and pickles. After I sell a house or two, I'll work more days and I can hire a maid, and we'll have money for steaks and cheesecake."

"A real maid, in a uniform and everything?"

"You're a nut—" Hal began, but we were interrupted by the tinkle of breaking glass. Mom had got so carried away by her project that she had forgotten Jennifer, who had sneaked into Mom's hideaway and was dropping things into the bathtub and sprinkling the shattered bits with talcum and soap powder.

Mom had also skipped her outing at the A & P, which may have been an outing for her, but I regarded it as sheer survival; and I wondered how she was going to break the news of her job to Dad over a lean and leftover dinner.

First, she softened him up with some mushroom

soup with wine in it, which I thought tasted terrible; then she put the tuna fish in a baking dish with crunched up Rice Chex and cheese on top, and that was pretty good. For dessert, we had a brown sugar and apple thing that was terrific.

Dad licked his chops and said, "Hmm, the cuisine is getting pretty fancy around here. What's up?"

He wasn't really suspicious; he was just being nice.

Mom launched out: "Well, I got to thinking if I got out more and talked to real people, not just Jennifer, my morale would be better and I wouldn't just slam cans and hot dogs on the table all the time."

Then she threw the fast ball. "So I thought I'd get a job."

"Hmm? Huh? What?" Dad choked over his coffee.

Mom got up and showed him the paper, and he stared at it for quite a while. "You think you're going to make enough to pay a keeper for Jennifer?"

"I'll only do it weekends to begin with—that's the busiest time, anyway. So Hal will be here, and after I've sold a house, I'll have money to hire a regular sitter."

Dad looked at Hal, and they both shook their heads gloomily. Dad said, "See what happened because you talked me into buying the local paper so you could look at the movies? You'll never get to go to a movie now."

75

"I don't blame Mom, really," said Hal. "I think she ought to get out someplace."

"Uh, Amy—" Dad cleared his throat. "You know, you need a license to sell real estate. You have to take an exam."

Mom stared, and you could see the whole project starting to collapse. She looked as if she might cry.

"Oh, why did we ever even *look* at houses? It was all a mistake. We should have stayed in New York."

"Now, Amy, you know we couldn't have stayed in that tiny apartment. Besides, I like it here."

"But at least in New York, I could get *out!* I didn't stay in the tiny apartment all day with Jennifer. It's all right for you—you get to go to New York every day."

"Lucky me. Look, hire a sitter one day at my expense and come into New York and meet me. You can buy a velvet gown and a mink hat, and I'll take you to dinner."

Mom looked less like crying. "All right. Thank you. But what I mean is, I miss all the people I used to talk to in the daytime. Like the park men, the nice one and the cross one, and old Mrs. Spinich who takes care of Barbara's baby, and Louie in the delicatessen—lots of people that I said hello to every day."

Dad said, "You'll make friends out here. Jennifer will get bigger and she won't tie you down so much."

Suddenly I saw what Mom meant. I missed all those people myself. "It's not friends exactly," I said to Dad. "Mom means people that you sort of look forward to seeing every day. It's a routine. Here you just see people disappearing in their station wagons."

"You ought to write a book, Berries," Dad kidded me. I remember now, he said that.

"Listen, Dad," I said, "couldn't we all go into New York one day? You know, for an outing, and to see everyone?"

"O.K., good idea."

"Not Jennifer," said Hal.

Hal and I started making plans, and Mom looked thoughtful. "That'll be fun, but a holiday isn't what I mean, and it isn't just getting to know more people. I don't really want to ask people for coffee or cocktails, and then have them ask us. I want something to *do*, in the daytime. Like in New York I went to the park, and the store, and the laundry, and the school, and there were certain people I talked to at each place."

She pushed back her chair and started to clear the table. "I'll bet I can get a real estate license. I'm not so dumb. I'll call up Miss Real Estate and ask her about it."

"We know a lot of people in New York who are always talking about moving to the suburbs," I said. "We can tell them all to come to Mom, and she'll sell lots of houses. Then we'll get rich, and we can join Sidney's club. They have a swimming pool and bowling alleys and ice cream in tall glasses with a cherry on top. He's going to take me pretty soon."

Hal started counting on his fingers. "Let's see, Mom's house money is going to buy steaks, a sitter, and now Sidney's club. She better sell plenty of houses."

"She'd better not sell this one out from under us, though, just to get back to New York," said Dad. Mom looked guilty, as if she had thought of doing just that.

Dad told Mom to go ahead and hire her sitter and bring me and Hal into the city that Friday. Hal made a date with an old girl of his that he called Kite String— her real name was Kate Strang. Mom called Irvy's mother, so I could go see him while she went shopping for the velvet gown.

We all met Dad at this Swedish restaurant, where there is a big table loaded with food, and you take your plate and go round as many times as you want, just helping yourself to cold meat and fish, and salad and pickles and olives and fruit, practically everything you can think of. Irvy and I didn't even have to wait till Mom and Dad finished their cocktails. By the time they ate, we were on our third trip. Dessert came separate— thin hot pancakes with jam. Irvy and I were really stuffed.

Mom hadn't bought a velvet gown or a mink hat. She got a salmon-colored suit and new shoes for selling real estate in. Dad hadn't got her headed off from that job.

She put on the new suit for us that night, and everyone whistled and I said, "Boy, you could sell a hotel in that!"

Hal said, "How're you going to get a job and sell houses when you're always being afraid even to call up a stranger?"

"That's why I have the new suit, to get my courage up," said Mom. "It's not so bad, though, calling people up for something definite, like getting a job or selling a house. It's calling them up for let's-be-friends that scares me."

The next morning, Mom went down to the agency to find out about the license. She came back and said it was all right; she could study for the exam and get the license later, and she was going to start work the next weekend.

"But that's the weekend I asked Kite to come out to go skating," said Hal.

"You can all go skating while Jennifer's taking her nap. Daddy'll be here."

"Sure," said Dad, "I'll take care of Jen while she's asleep. Glad to."

"Yeah, Kite and I'll be stuck with her awake and raging! I can hardly wait till I go away to college."

Kite was the first overnight visitor we'd had, and Mom made me clear out the attic room Sandra and I had been using for a rainy day clubhouse. I didn't mind too much, because I liked Kite. She was better than any of the girls Hal had brought home from school. They just goggled and giggled, which was pretty embarrassing to have going on right in your own kitchen. It bothered Mom, too—she kept retreating to her hideaway to read.

Kite was really good looking: tall, black hair, and straight black eyebrows over very bright eyes. Her face was very white, with sort of a deadpan lack of expression to begin with, but Mom said this was just because she was scared of other people. Mom liked her, and Kite loosened up pretty fast and sat around the kitchen, nibbling on cereal and pickles just like one of us.

Hal had picked Kite up from the train Friday afternoon, and after a while they had gone off somewhere. Late in the afternoon I finished a book I was reading about a kid whose experiments were always blowing up, and I went down into the kitchen. Sitting on the two kitchen stools were Kite and Sandra.

"Why didn't you yell?" I said to Sandra. "I was just upstairs reading."

She hardly glanced at me, she was so busy telling Kite all about the one-hundred-yard freestyle swimming race she won last summer. Kite told her about racing Sailfish on Long Island Sound. (We used to go out to Long Island in the summer, when we lived in New York. That's where Hal met Kite.) They sounded as if they'd been talking for ages. Sandra sure got acquainted fast.

"Where is everyone?" I said finally.

Kite said, "I think your mother went to get your father, and Hal went upstairs to see a lady about a swordfish."

Sandra's eyes popped. She never knew when someone was kidding.

"He's probably changing his clothes, stupid," I explained to her. Then I asked Kite, "Are you and him going out again?"

"Are you and *he*—" Sandra butted in.

"Go soak your head!" I said. She just winked at Kite, as if *they* were sharing a joke, and I got ready to paste her.

"Where do we go skating tomorrow?" Kite asked, getting the conversation back to neutral.

"Down at the pond by the town rec field," I said. "Can you play hockey?"

"No, but I do absolutely Olympic figure eights."

"Are you really going to be in the Olympics?" Sandra asked. "I bet I could learn to do a figure eight too, if you taught me."

"O.K.," said Kite good-naturedly.

"You mean I can come?" Sandra pinned her down fast.

"You've got to ask Hal," I said.

Of course by the time he came downstairs and she asked him, he figured it was all settled. He probably thought Sandra and I would go off and leave them alone, too, but it didn't work out that way.

Driving down to the pond the next day, Sandra hung over the back of the front seat, asking Kite all kinds of questions about sailing and school and her family. Kite's naturally polite, so she asked Sandra about her family. She got a big blast about Sandra's stuck-up older sister, who is going to be a debutante. Sandra was chattering as if someone had thrown the stopper away. I don't think anyone in her own family had ever exchanged three whole sentences with her.

Hal looked bored, and I tied a few knots in Sandra's skate laces. Kite untied them for her later.

The kids my age were playing hockey down at one end of the pond, so I went down there, but Sandra didn't come along. Usually she was the only girl that played, and we had to let her because she could skate better than most of us. Sidney was there, though, and he and I made two goals. Every now and again, when we'd lost the puck, I looked over and Hal and Kite were doing figures, and Sandra was tagging along right beside them. I bet Hal was furious.

After a while the older boys wanted to play hockey and shoved us kids off. Kite was sitting on the bank resting, and I went over with Sidney and introduced him.

"I saw you doing eights," he said. "I'd have brought my figure skates if I'd known anyone that good would be here."

"I saw you shooting goals. You looked pretty good too," Kite said.

Sandra had to butt in. "I use the *same* skates for figures and hockey."

"Anyone *can* play hockey in figure skates like yours. My mom doesn't want me to," Sidney said.

Sandra sniffed. Sidney's brother Marty came by just then, and he had to go home.

Looking after them, Sandra said, "I don't know why they have to come here. Why don't they go skate with their friends on the pond over near Hebrew Heaven?"

Nobody answered, and old steamroller Sandra pushed on. "That's what my mother calls Olcott Acres, where they live. It's all Jewish over there."

Still silence, and I suddenly thought maybe Kite was Jewish. That dumb Sandra. It was lucky Hal was playing hockey, or he'd have bashed her.

Kite didn't seem embarrassed. She just said, "What of it? I'm Jewish too."

Sandra looked as if she'd said she had two heads. "You're not!"

"I am. At least my father is. My mother's a hillbilly from West Virginia." Kite winked at me and added, "She never even wore shoes till she was twelve."

Sandra ignored that and clutched at straws. "You're not really then, only part. Sidney's all. They even belong to a special club, awfully expensive, and just Jewish."

"Sure, sure, and they all drive Cadillacs and wear diamonds and use mink bathmats, don't they?"

"Uh . . . ?"

Kite laughed. "Child, you must learn not to believe everything you hear."

"See, we told you you talk like a Nazi," I said.

"Oh, shut up! You don't know anything." Sandra looked at Kite cautiously. "What kind of a car do you have?"

"We don't have any car at all." Then Kite pulled off her gloves and spread her hands out, palms down, and exclaimed, "Oh, my soul and little white body, I

84

musta left me diamonds on the train! Oh, well, I'll get a new set."

Slowly, slowly, Sandra broke into a smile. "You're kidding!"

"*That's* right! Now, the next time you hear all that stuff about minks and Cadillacs, remember me, an ordinary person."

Sandra wrinkled up her nose and hunched her shoulders. "I'm freezing. Let's quit talking, and run around. I know, we can play follow the leader. I'm leader!"

She hopped around the edge of the pond, alternating with skips and double jumps, and I followed her with Kite behind me. At the lower end of the pond the outlet is fenced off. The ice is apt to be weak there, and anyway there's a big drop below the dam, so you're not supposed to go past the fence. Sandra put her hand on a fence post and vaulted over.

"Hey, you're not allowed in there!" I said.

"Baby! Just because you can't do it."

I managed to scramble over and of course Kite vaulted neatly. Sandra hopped to the edge of the outlet. There were walls built on each side and the overflow from the dam dropped quite a ways, maybe ten or fifteen feet, and then ran through a big culvert pipe. Sandra got ready to jump.

85

I yelled, "You're crazy! I'm not going to jump that!"

"Baby! Look, Kite, I can fly like a kite!" She ran two steps and jumped. She cleared it, but not by much.

Kite walked to the edge and looked down. She shook her head. "You shouldn't do that; it's too dangerous. If you even slipped a bit . . ."

Just then Hal grabbed me by the collar and shook me. "You dumb kids, you know you're not allowed in here! Get back over that fence, Berries. Sandra, you climb over the fence on that side and walk back across the ice. Of all the jerky—"

"I'm sorry, I should have stopped her," said Kite.

"You couldn't have known. But *she* knew." Hal shoved me so hard I fell down climbing over the fence, and then he went and grabbed Sandra and started really scolding her. She looked pretty scared for once.

"I'll never bring *you* again, you big dumb show-off!" Hal finished up.

"I wasn't showing off. It's not that hard. I've seen other kids do it, lots of times. Big kids."

"Well, don't you do it, not ever, hear me?"

"O.K. I'm sorry. I made it though, easy."

"Quit boasting!" Hal snapped. Sandra seemed a little subdued finally. She and I sat quietly in the back seat on the way home, and Hal and Kite talked about some movie with a French title. We got home, and Sandra stood looking at Kite like a dog begging for a bite of toast.

"Are you coming out to go skating again some-day?" she asked.

"Sure, I guess so," said Kite.

" 'Bye, Sandra," Hal said, in case she had any ideas of coming in.

Soulfully, Sandra said to Kite, "Good-bye."

She went home, and Kite said, "It's funny how a kid can be a pain in the neck but you still sort of like her, isn't it?"

"Huh!" said Hal.

7

Mavis

You wouldn't think anyone could really have a name
like that, but she did: Mavis Funk. Since the day she
came it's gotten to be an expression in our family. If
Mom is trying to steamroller Dad into taking a trip or
buying a sofa or something, he'll say, "Quit trying to
Mavis me!"

Mavis came with the spring. What happened was
that when the weather got all balmy and lilac-smelling,
the city people began streaming out to the suburbs to
look at houses. Mom was on the phone all the time,
either to owners or customers or the office. Reporting
back to the office, her conversation would sound like
this:

"Hitchcock adores Quincy. They won't even look

at anything else. Quincy is ready to take Youngstown, but they can't get a mortgage, and Youngstown wants cash right away because he's already closed on Bannerman. Hitchcock will wind up going to New Jersey, I just know it. They have a grandmother there."

Hitchcock did, too, and Mom made more phone calls. Dad opened the phone bill and said, "Is this a business, or a phone company benefit?"

But all of a sudden, Quincy's great-uncle died and left him the money, and he bought Youngstown. Dad said, "What d'you know, all this time I thought Youngstown was a city in Ohio!"

It was Mom's first sale, and she got $1,250, which was two and a half percent of the purchase price. You can figure it out for yourself—it's the way I learned how to do fractions. Mom knew by heart what was two and a half percent of the price of every house for sale in town.

She came home that night looking as if she had wings. "It's not just the money. It's—it's *doing* it. Imagine, I sold a house! Me."

Dad groaned. "Now it'll get worse. You won't be happy till you've sold another."

He was right, but Mom was lucky. An old college friend of hers turned up, who had two girls in high school and was just about to have a new baby, and Mom sold her an expensive big house with an apple orchard for the friend and a good commission for Mom.

One night Hal said, "How about all those steaks and baby-sitters we were going to have when you made your fortune?"

"Hmm," said Mom, and she reached in her pocketbook and pulled out ten dollars as if it was nothing. "Go down and buy an enormous thick T-bone steak!"

Hal whistled and shot out the door. We celebrated on the steak all right, and two days later Mom came home with Mavis.

I had come home from school and fed Spooky. I was just heading out to play when I saw Spooky had made a mess in the living room again. The shovel was still upstairs from the last time, and I didn't want to bother getting it. I grabbed a piece of cardboard and wrote "Detour" on it in large letters and set it over Spooky's mistake. Spooky and I admired it and then we went out.

A while later I saw Mom drive up, and with her was this character about twice Mom's size, dressed in a navy blue overcoat like a policewoman. The character followed Mom into the house, and I slid in behind them.

Hal had Jennifer in the kitchen sink, pretty much bare. There was a pile of Jen's dirty clothes on the floor,

90

smelling wildly of perfume and talcum powder. Evidently she'd got loose in Mom's hideaway again.

"Sorry, Mom," said Hal, looking like a half-corked volcano. He glared at me and went on: "*He* left Spooky's mess in the living room and I stepped in it, and while I was cleaning that up, Jen got away from me."

"Didn't you see my sign?"

Hal scowled and started to say more, but Mom was speaking.

"Boys, this is Mrs. Funk. This is Hal, my eldest son, with Jennifer. And Bertrand—we all call him Berries. Boys, Mrs. Funk is coming to . . . uh, help us out. With Jennifer."

Hal was trying to hold Jennifer with his left hand and hold out his right to Mrs. Funk, and Jennifer got a saucepan and dumped water all over his feet. I snickered.

Mrs. Funk fixed me with the policewoman's eye. "The children may call me Mavis. Bertrand, there is no reason for laughter. Your brother is doing his best. Kindly hand me that apron behind you, and I will take over."

I handed, and she took over, all right. I tried to fade out the back door, but Hal was right after me, and he really gave it to me that time.

I didn't come back in till I figured it must be suppertime.

Mavis had the table set with two places and a high chair in position for Jennifer.

"She won't sit in that," I informed Mavis.

"Time to wash our hands," said Mavis. It was my first taste of the royal "We."

She set Jennifer on the kitchen stool by the sink, and Jen actually washed instead of splashing and held out her hands to be toweled like a little doll.

"We're nice and clean," said Mavis. She popped Jen into the high chair and snapped on the tray. I expected howls of rage.

"Nicenkeen!" said Jen, a talking doll. I stared.

"Come along, Bertrand, we mustn't let our dinner get cold!"

I moved slowly to the table, where the two places seemed to be for me and Mavis. There was some fat on the meat, which I picked off and stuck on the table.

"We use our knife and fork, Bertrand," said Mavis.

"I don't need a knife, it's cut, and my name is Berries."

"Use your fork then . . . Berries." She said my nickname as if it tasted bad. "Jennifer may use a spoon. She is only three."

Jen had eaten half her meat, which was pretty good for her. She held out a piece to Spooky, who was waiting as usual. Mavis picked Spooky up and dumped her out the back door.

"Hey, my dog—" I started.

"We must clean our plates before we have dessert," Mavis rolled on. She spooned up a mixture of potato and beans and put it in Jen's mouth, and Jen actually swallowed it.

Boy, if she tries that on me, she'll find out, I thought. Aloud I said, "What's for dessert?"

"We'll see when we're finished," said Mavis.

"Look, I may not even *want* any. What is it?"

Mavis just went on feeding Jennifer, and when she was done she put a bowl of Jello in front of her.

"I hate Jello," I said and pushed my chair back.

"We don't ask to be excused till everyone is finished," said Mavis.

Funny thing is, I didn't quite dare say "nuts to you" and get up. I sat. I didn't ask to be excused, though. When Mavis put Jennifer down, I got up and went to find Mom.

"Hey, *listen*," I said, when I found her upstairs, "this Mavis is impossible. I'm not going to eat with her."

"Oh, yes, you are," said Mom. "Or starve."

"Count on Berries to avoid that," said Dad.

"Listen, she won't even let my dog in the house. My own dog. Who does she think she is?"

"She's the boss," said Mom. "And take the fire shovel downstairs."

Disgusted, I went down to watch TV. Mom and Dad and Hal sat down to dinner, and after a bit Mavis brought Jennifer in, all pink and white and brushed and pajamaed.

"We've come to say good night," said Mavis.

"Goo' ni'," said Jennifer, offering a cheek to be kissed, first to Mom and then to Dad. They stared at each other.

"She's tame," said Dad. "This is the millenium."

"I'll call Berries for his bath, as soon as I'm ready," said the tyrant.

"I don't need a bath!" I yelped.

"We *will* have a bath," said Mavis.

I saw the opening and sneered, "What d'you mean, *we?*"

Hal snickered, but Dad turned traitor on me. He said, "Go take your bath, and mind your manners too."

Mavis sailed upstairs and I slunk after. I went into the bathroom and locked the door, in case Mavis had any ideas of coming in to wash me. Besides, I needed privacy to plot my revenge.

Mavis didn't work for us Mondays and Tuesdays. She went home. So the first Wednesday morning, when she came back, I had a pail of water rigged over the door to her room. Mom had made me clean it all up and paint out the sign on the door that said: BLACK HAND SOCIETY—DEATH TO TRAITORS.

Mavis must have had experience, because she spotted the pail before it spilled on her. She made me haul the ladder all the way up from the cellar again to take the pail down.

Next I made sure her gloves dropped on the floor, so Spooky chewed them. Mom made a rule that I would have to pay for anything Spooky chewed. Hal promptly took fifty cents off me when she chewed an old no-good belt that he never wore anyway. Come to think, I'll bet he gave it to her, just so he could collect. I was even more determined on revenge.

I consulted Sandra, and she said her father had some special slow-drying glue. She swiped it for me, and I poured some in Mavis's shoes before I went to school one Wednesday morning.

I sure wish I'd been there when she put them on. It must have been a treat—she had both shoes on before she found out, and then she could hardly get them off. Of course Dad made me pay for the shoes and stockings, which took most of my allowance all year. I guess it was worth it, though.

That was about as far as I got with revenge. I gave up after that. Mavis was part English and part German and all stubborn; she never gave up on anything. I took Hal's advice: "Use strategy, play her along, and you'll have her eating out of your hand."

Actually, I was eating out of hers, because she started bringing pies from home on Wednesdays and making cookies at our house. I mean, after all, you might as well say "May I be excused" if it pays off in pies.

We ate awfully well while Mavis was with us, because she always asked Mom what was for dinner right after breakfast, and she had the idea there ought to be real meat and vegetables and dessert every night, not just on special occasions, which was the way Mom looked at it.

Mom got so rattled trying to think up what was for dinner before she'd hardly had her coffee, that one afternoon she sat down and wrote up a schedule: lamb chops and spinach on Wednesday, hamburger and beans on Thursday, fish on Friday, roast something on Saturday, and leftover roast something on Sunday. Mondays and Tuesdays, when we were on our own, we reverted to finding something after hunger set in.

Mavis liked having the menus the same each day of the week, but Dad said he liked to wonder what surprise he'd get at home, such as Curried Illusion of

Lamb, or Goodman Surprise Pie. So he and Mom and Hal went on eating those things, and I got the lamb chops with Mavis and Jennifer. Hal drooled with envy.

Mavis made the world go round for Jennifer, and my little terror of a sister became a changed character. She'd learned to talk in real words and she stopped screaming and hurling herself on the floor. I guess all along she just wanted someone to tell her the score, and Mavis told her, all right.

Spooky followed Mavis around too. It really broke me up when I came home from school one day, and Spooky didn't even come jump on me. She just sat and watched Mavis molding hamburgers. A dog always knows who runs the kitchen—a kid doesn't really have a chance to own his own dog. Of course Mavis also fed Spooky when I forgot, which was pretty often, and she took her for walks when she went out with Jennifer. Oh, well, Spooky still slept on the end of my bed.

So there we all were, settled in the suburbs with a dog and a maid, and Dad had his garden all ready to plant in the right place this time, and Hal was chairman of the Junior Prom. We all got to arguing about whether we ought to buy the house.

I was in favor of staying at Olcott Corners for keeps, but of course nobody paid much attention to me. The rest of the family liked Olcott all right, but they couldn't get right down to buying the house. Mom said, how did she know, she might see a house she liked better. Hal said it didn't make much difference to him, he'd be away soon, but how were we going to afford a house and college at the same time?

"A very good point," said Dad. "I should have inherited a rich ancestor years ago, but it's too late to begin now."

"I might sell Auchincloss," said Mom. "They're asking eighty-five thousand dollars, and at two and a half percent, that's . . ."

"You believe it," said Dad.

The arguments drifted along and we didn't buy the house; we went on renting. This family doesn't make decisions much, unless they're very sudden ones.

8

Passover

With Mavis home to mind Jennifer, Mom didn't mind driving me around to visit other kids. She took me to a Passover party with Sidney at his club, and it was a really good party. There was plenty of cake and candy and sodas and prizes for the little kids. The big kids and grown-ups played something called The Game. One person acts out a word or sentence, and the rest of his team tries to guess it. I didn't try to play, but Sidney was good at it.

After the party, Hal picked me up, and we gave Sidney a ride home too, because his family had a lot of other guests to carry. Hal had a new girl with him. I suppose she was his age, but she sure didn't look it; she was tiny. She also had her hair cut short, almost like a boy's.

Hal said, "Lyle, this is my kid brother, Berries, and this is Sidney Fine. Lyle Cope."

She cocked her head on one side and said, "Hiya, Berries," as if we were old pals. I grunted.

Sidney put his hand right out and said, "How do you do, Miss Cope?"

She looked at him. She cocked her head on the other side and her eyes flicked over the entrance to the club and back to Sidney.

She said, "How do you do, Mr. Fine? How're things in the Land of Milk and Honey?"

"All right," said Sidney, looking wary. He knew as well as I did that a high-school kid wouldn't ordinarily call him Mr. Fine. There was something phony about the way she was talking; maybe it was just meant to impress Hal. It makes you sore when people talk over your head that way, the way grown-ups do in French sometimes.

"There wasn't any milk and honey anyway," I said. "There was cake and plenty of sodas."

This Lyle girl giggled, and Sidney and I turned around and looked out the back window and talked baseball. When we got to Sidney's house, a bunch of kids were playing baseball outside, and he yelled that he'd be right out to play as soon as he changed his clothes.

Hal turned the car around and I looked back at the kids. "I wish we'd bought a house here. There are never enough kids for a baseball game around our place."

Lyle turned to me and raised her eyebrows and shoulders. "Oi! Oi! You want to be one of the Chosen People?"

I grunted and her eyes slid around to see if Hal was laughing. He looked embarrassed and said, "I don't think Berries catches on."

Lyle said, "My, my, I must explain the facts of life to him. Well, Berries, you couldn't buy a house in Olcott Acres, because it's all Jewish."

"We could too! We almost did. You must be just about as dumb as Sandra."

"Who's Sandra?"

"She's a girl. She thinks that Jews all have to live in one part of town. She's off her rocker—you can ask Hal."

Lyle cocked her head at Hal. He muttered, "Sandra's that bossy squirt that lives next to us. She and Berries are always arguing."

The big fink! He wouldn't tell this Lyle squirt off the way he did Sandra. Teen-age kids can be even worse than grown-ups. They're always trying to make it look

101

as if little kids don't know anything. Hal and Lyle made a big show of talking very grown-up about some book, and I sat back and grouched.

I was glad to get home and change out of my fancy pants, and then I went to find Sandra. I guess it was a Saturday afternoon, because her father was home, watching some game on television. As I said before, you never can be sure whether he's going to be full of jokes or going to snap your head off.

"Excuse me," I said politely, not taking any chances, "is Sandra around?"

"Little old Sandra Pigtails?" he boomed. He seemed to be in a good mood. He shouted toward the kitchen, "Adelaide, where's Sandra?"

"I think she's upstairs sulking because Berries went to a Passover party." Her voice got louder as she came toward the living room. Then she came in and saw me and her voice changed. "Oh, hello, Berries. Run up and see if Sandra is in her room."

I went up and found Sandra, and we played with a new maze game she had, until Mrs. Graham called to us that we ought to go out. Mr. Graham had turned off the TV and was standing by the fireplace. He was clinking the ice around in his drink.

He called, "All cheered up now, Pigtails? The Children of Israel didn't get Berries after all, did they?"

"Un-uh."

He beckoned to me. "Come over here, boy. You really like that fancy club, huh? Like the smell of all that money in the Promised Land?"

He tried to put his hand on my shoulder, as if we were pals kidding together. I yanked away.

"I just like my friend, that's all!" I bumped into Sandra and shoved out the door. As I slammed it behind me, I heard Mr. Graham booming and chuckling away to himself. Sandra followed me outside and sort of stood there, not looking at me.

I exploded. "Who does he think he is, making those cracks? I'm not going to talk to your father again, ever! If he asks me something, I'm not going to answer."

"He just kids around like that," Sandra said apologetically. We threw the ball a bit and she said, "Sidney's your best friend at school. I'm your best friend at home, right?"

"Well, you happen to be the only kid around here," I said, and she had to be satisfied with that.

At dinner I was waiting for Dad to cut up the chicken, which takes him a very long time—I don't know why he doesn't give up and let Hal do it—and I said, "Are there more Jewish people living in Olcott Corners than in New York?"

Dad stared at me. "Goodness, no! There are very few in Olcott and millions in New York."

He went on rending the chicken, and I could *feel* the mashed potatoes getting too cold to melt the butter. Finally he got us all served out, and he said, "What's the trouble, Berries? You still fretting because you don't get out of school here for the Jewish holidays?"

"It's not that. I hardly ever *heard* of Jews when we lived in New York. Out here people keep making all these jokes about Hebrew Heaven and stuff like that. I don't get it."

"Just clucks making bad jokes."

"What's the joke about the people at Sidney's club? They're just ordinary people."

Dad said, "Some people are prejudiced. That means they dislike another whole group of people without there being any sensible reason for it."

I turned to Hal. "See, that girl of yours is a cluck and a prejudiced, too!"

Hal snapped, "You pick your girls, and I'll pick mine."

"What girl is this?" Mom asked. She's always curious about Hal's girls.

"Her name's Lyle Cope. I just met her at the Country Club dance. She's really cute and . . . well, interesting."

"Huh, *I* thought she was *dumb!* You told Sandra off when she was talking about Olcott Acres being all Jewish, but you wouldn't tell that Lyle cluck."

Dad put down his knife and fork. "What *is* this all about?"

Hal explained. "It was weeks ago. Sandra was showing off as usual, and she said Jewish people weren't allowed to buy houses on this street or go to Olcott Corners school, something like that. So I told her she was nuts."

"Didn't tell Lyle, though—" I started, but Dad gave me a look. He and Mom looked at each other a moment.

Sort of slowly, Mom said, "There isn't any law, of course. But, for instance, in the real estate business I'm not supposed to sell a house in this part of town to Jewish people."

"Why not?"

"Well, I don't know. It's sort of an agreement."

"How can you tell who's Jewish?"

"I can't, really. I sort of talk around and get their references and friends' names and where they go to church. That's what Miss Real Estate was doing when we first came out, and Irvy Weinstein and his bag of bagels was with us. So she only showed us houses in Olcott Acres and Indian Road."

Hal stared at Mom. "Do *you* do that, too?"

"I hope I don't act as dopey as she did. But I do try to find out and steer Jewish people away from the restricted areas."

105

"I think that sounds rotten," said Hal. "What if you didn't do it?"

"The agency wouldn't let me work there anymore. All the agencies do it. There are some Jewish salesmen too, and they do the same."

I asked, "What about the school business? Sandra keeps saying Sidney sneaked into our school; he's not meant to be there."

"The rest of Olcott Acres isn't in our school district," Mom said. "Mr. Fine lived there first, before he built the development, and his kids came to our school. Then they changed the district line so all the people from that development wouldn't come to the village school."

"Because they didn't want them?"

"Well—they said the school would be too crowded."

"Aren't there any other Jewish children in our school?"

"There's Joe Pearl. His father came by himself when they bought their house in the village, because his mother looks very Jewish."

"How can she *look* it?"

"A good many Jewish people have very dark hair and prominent noses. Like a lot of Swedes are very blond and blue-eyed."

"If this Joey Pearl is Jewish, he must be a dope. He

didn't even take the holiday when it was Rosh Hashanah."

Dad gave me an odd, long look and pitched his napkin on the table. He said, "I'm going out for some air."

I couldn't tell if he was disgusted, or what. Since I've grown up, I've discovered Mom and Dad don't really like to talk about anything that's too serious or personal, especially not Dad. If there's something he can do, he'll do it, and when he's away sometimes he writes me sort of philosophical letters. This night in Olcott Corners I was sure disgusted and confused. I still didn't see why there was so much commotion about this Jewish business, and I didn't like people making cracks about my friend Sidney and his club.

So he'd know I was his friend, I went and called him up, and we had a long talk about baseball and some dumb girls at school.

9

Lyle

This Lyle character began to take over Hal's life. He got all moony about her, so he was always in a daze and didn't hear what I said, or if he did hear me he just snapped at me. He wouldn't even consider dropping me off somewhere if he was in the car with Lyle.

All in all, this second summer didn't turn out much livelier than the first one. I knew more kids in town, but if Mom wasn't driving around selling real estate, Hal had the car. I got nowhere. Sidney was around in July and used to come get me, but in August he went to visit his grandmother. Then Sandra and I stumped around and looked at the pond, which was full of green slime, and we sat in the treehouse and made plots about nothing. Spooky didn't even want to play; she just dug a hole in the dirt on the shady side of the house and slept.

I didn't see a whole lot of this Lyle, because she wasn't the type for hanging around the house to help with the dishes. Hal didn't actually see her very often either. She was mostly at the Country Club winning tennis tournaments, and we weren't members. Hal could only go to the club once a month as a guest, so he spent a lot of time thinking up projects for him and Lyle, so as to get her away from the Country Club crowd.

Some friends of ours gave a big Fourth of July dance, so he invited her to that. Sandra and I went to the early part of the party. Most of the girls had on these filmy, gauzy dresses, all in light colors. You know what Lyle's dress was made of? Denim—the stuff they make blue jeans of! She was really a cluck. She was always cocking her head and looking up at the boys with that phony sparrow look, and they really fell for it. Sandra and I maneuvered a plate of vanilla ice cream around, trying to plant it in a chair where Lyle was going to sit, but we never made it. Mom made us go home at eleven anyway.

Hal had a job at the newsstand and had to be there at seven o'clock every morning. Maybe that's one reason he was so grouchy. He figured the newsstand at dawn was better than being a caddy at the Country Club, when Lyle and all her friends were members. On

Thursdays he always went to Lyle's house to help her baby-sit her little brother, Thursday being the maid's day out. By all accounts the brother was the kind of monster that would make our Jen look like an angel, and Hal spent most of the afternoon horseying him around on his shoulders.

One Friday I heard Hal on the phone, asking Lyle to go bicycling with him, and he got turned down.

"Yah, she just goes with you if it's a really hot party, or she has nothing better to do," I said. "Like me and Sandra."

"Go play with Sandra and quit listening to my phone calls!" he yelled, and started punching me. Mavis came and looked at us, and Hal sloped off. Thank goodness for Mavis.

Toward the end of the summer Dad came home one night and said, "All the guys on the train are worried they're going to get hauled into their dress suits and dragged to some big community dance. Labor Day night, of all times. There's going to be a sit-down strike."

Of course Mom didn't know anything about it. Hal explained. "A bunch of the mothers of us poor but honest public school kids wants us to get integrated with those private school and Country Club characters. You know, in the lovely summertime we should all be friends together. So there's going to be a great ball on the Vil-

110

lage Green. Johnny Dempsey and his orchestra, even."

Dad said, "You get integrated. I'll stay home in my shorts and harvest tomatoes."

"O.K. if I take the car?"

"Take it. Wash it, even."

Hal called up Lyle to invite her. "This is Prince Goodman, and I'm inviting Cinderella to go to the ball with me in my Oldsmobile pumpkin."

Apparently this fruity line worked, because he talked a while and hung up looking pleased.

Hal was on the dance committee, of course, so the week before Labor Day he was out all the time, organizing bands and creampuffs and Japanese lanterns. A few days before the dance, Lyle telephoned him and he was out. She called the next day too, and both times I forgot to tell him.

Labor Day morning she telephoned, and she had that real peeved, fake grown-up tone to her voice: "Could I *please* speak to Hal?"

I remembered then that I hadn't told him about the earlier calls, and I had a feeling I was going to catch it. The conversation from Hal's end was hard to follow, except I could tell for sure things were going wrong.

Hal said, "Hello, hello, hello! Lovable Labor Day! . . . You phoned when? . . . Honest, nobody told me."

I ducked behind the sofa as Hal looked around angrily. He went on: "No one ever tells me anything

111

around here, honestly. What's the big deal, anyway? I'll see you tonight. What time— . . . You *what?*"

There was a long silence at our end, while she talked. Hal groaned and started protesting. "You can't . . . Listen, I know your grandfather's a nice old gent, but he doesn't care about his birthday. Tell him you promised. . . . You couldn't have mixed up the date, it's Labor Day—"

She started talking again, and Hal tried to interrupt several times but never quite made it. Then he was perfectly quiet, listening, and he started blushing, dark red, even up the back of his neck.

He said, "O.K., Lyle, you don't have to make up any more stories. I get the picture, and I can hear all your friends snickering there. Have an absolute ball with dear old Grandpa, will you? I bet you don't even *have* a grandfather!" He slammed the phone down and lunged out the back door.

He went to the dance alone—you could hear the tires hiss as he gunned the car out of the driveway—and he looked pretty grim for a few days. Finally, when we were sitting in the kitchen, eating apples, I got my courage up and said, "Sorry I forgot those phone calls from that . . . uh . . . girl."

Hal took an extra large snapping bite out of his apple and then he said, "It wouldn't have made any difference if you'd remembered, not really."

"Did you get someone else to go to the dance with you?"

"Nah."

"Her grandfather have a party the same night or something?"

Hal had been sitting placidly on the kitchen counter, so I was startled when he yanked me off my stool and started yelling, "You quit listening to my phone calls and don't tell anyone about them!" He got in a few good punches before I wriggled free.

That was the end of our second—the last, it turned out to be—summer at Olcott Corners. It had been pretty much of a drag. Once Dad took us all to Fire Island to swim, and I had fun, but he kept wishing we still had a boat. All winter he used to plan boat trips he'd take.

That's what was wrong with our summers in Olcott—we didn't have a change to look forward to all winter.

10

Accident

I had two good friends at school that next year. A new kid joined the class, named Jack Rumble—really—and he teamed up with me and Sidney, and we had a war with two big kids in the sixth grade. I bet Sandra sicked them onto us.

At first they just made corny cracks about our names, like "Here come Fine Rumbles and Raspberries." Then they found out they could always reach Sidney by grabbing his cap or one of his books and hiding it. The thing is, Sidney's mother checked up on all his things, so pretty soon she'd come swooping down to complain to the teacher or even the principal. She seemed to think kids were picking on Sidney specially.

Of course the kids thought Sidney was a tattletale and they liked all this commotion with his mother, so then they picked on him more.

The two kids who were our main enemies were bigger than us, but there were three of us and only two of them. Still, if we got into a fight, it didn't work out. Sidney was too little, and Jack was tall and skinny and awkward. I didn't mind getting punched—I was used to it from Hal—but I didn't want to get slaughtered.

Jack said we couldn't get anywhere without strategy. He brought flour and put it in this kid's gym shoes, so it flew out in a cloud, and the gym teacher thought he'd done it for a gag and chewed him out. The kid got even by cutting holes in Jack's sneakers; then we spent the weekend collecting burrs to put inside his shorts.

We spent most of every Saturday planning the next offensive, and usually the best place to plan was in our treehouse. It made Sandra pretty mad, as she was left out. She was used to dealing with just Sidney and me.

With the three of us up there, first she tried to persuade us to come down and play a game with two on each side. Sidney and Jack wouldn't bite. Then she yelled that they weren't allowed in the treehouse and she was going to come out at night and kill the tree with weed killer.

"Yah, it won't work," Jack answered, "Anyway, you know what? We're building a tunnel under your

115

house, and we're going to blow it up. On Christmas. No toys for you!"

I added, "You better go home and play with your dolls while you've got a chance!"

That really made her mad because she hated dolls anyway. Her voice trembled. "Just you wait! I saw Spooky eating some funny looking meat, and I bet it was poisoned."

Sandra ran home and I worried some about Spooky, but she acted all right. I bet Sandra just made that up.

After that, Sandra used to leave me threatening letters in the treehouse, and we answered with weirder threats. When I got tired of that, I wrote her that I heard her father say he wasn't going to get her a pony, ever; he was going to get her a hair-dressing set, so she could take her hair out of pigtails and curl it. She waited till she caught me alone and beat up on me after that. She'd gotten a lot bigger than me.

When Christmas vacation came, Jack was sick with the flu and the treehouse plotting stopped. Sandra came back and started bossing me around extra, to make up for lost time. She really seemed a lot older now, and even if Sidney was around we both gave up and let her do the organizing.

We were outside one day, trying to teach Spooky to retrieve sticks. Spooky just ran with them, and we chased. Accidentally on purpose, Sandra ran into Sidney and knocked him down. He tore a hole in his pants. They were new pants and he looked really upset and went inside to find Mavis.

"Tattletale, tattle! Go get a rattle!" Sandra chanted after him. I didn't join in, but I wished he wouldn't get Mavis stirred up. We were standing there, practicing to look innocent if Mavis came out, when Hal drove up. He had a girl with him—Kite String. I hadn't seen her for a year.

Sandra practically swooned. She said, "Hello-o-o!" and her mouth and her eyes were round.

"Gee, hi! I didn't know you were coming," I said.

"Yeah, I actually pulled off one whole phone call without you listening!" said Hal.

Sandra said, "Can we all go skating again?"

Mavis came outside with Sidney just then, with a pair of my pants roped up around his middle, and a determined look in her eye.

Hal groaned. "Not *three* of these monsters! We're outnumbered!"

Mavis said, "Berries, I think it's time for your friends to go home. There's too much quarreling. I can't have all this trouble with Jennifer sick."

"Good! Send 'em all home," said Hal. "We can take Berries—if we *have* to."

"I guess I'll go home and read one of my Christmas books," said Sandra brokenly. She started home, dragging her feet and waiting for someone to call her back.

"May I call my mother, please?" Sidney said. He looked embarrassed, the way he did if anything went wrong.

"Hal, I don't really mind if we take them all," said Kite. "We'll shoo them all down to one end, and I'll only have eyes for you."

"I'll bet!" Hal groaned, but with Mavis standing like a post in the door and everyone else looking gloomy, he gave up. Sandra broke for home and was back with her skates before I'd even found my socks. We three kids got in the back, and Kite sang us verses of "You Can't Get to Heaven" that I'd never heard before. It started off like a nice, jolly afternoon.

We stopped by Sidney's house for his skates. He made sure he got his figure skates this time. His mother waved from the door. "Have a good time!" To Sidney she added, "Take care, now!"

"I'm *always* careful," Sidney told her, which was true.

A good kids' hockey game was going on at the end of the pond, so they didn't have any trouble getting rid of *me*. Sidney and Sandra were something else again. Now they both had their figure skates on, each of them was determined to impress Kite with the fanciest figure.

I could hear their yells: "Watch me! Lookit this!" Hal swooped down to my end of the pond and gave me a dirty look. It wasn't *my* fault.

I guess he finally decided it was impossible to get Sandra and Sidney away from Kite, so he took her away. They went to this joint the teen-agers call The I-Ball, where they get Cokes and coffee, and play records. There were plenty of people at the pond, grown-ups and children, and the ice was safe all over—no thin places anyone could fall in. Hal said they'd be back to pick us up in a little while.

Sidney got into the hockey game. The sides had been uneven, and he asked first; once he was in, neither team would let the other have Sandra, so she was left out.

We played till kids started drifting home, or their parents came for them. Several people offered us a ride, but Sandra said, "No thank you, we have to wait for Kite and Hal. They might be worried." I didn't think they'd be worried, and I was getting awfully cold.

"Do you think they're in love?" said Sandra. "People in love always forget what time it is."

"Nah. When he was in love he acted awfully grouchy."

Sidney said, "Let's take off our skates and play leapfrog, before our toes freeze."

We did, but our toes still froze.

"If you walk on your hands, your feet get warm," Sidney said. He probably just said it because he's so good at it, and he walked all over on his hands while Sandra kept doing two steps and falling down. I couldn't stand on my hands at all.

Sandra turned a few cartwheels, down toward the end of the pond. She stood there a second, looking at the outlet. She turned around. Sidney was still walking on his hands, as if he could do it all day.

Sandra shouted: "Bet you can't jump the outlet! I dare you!"

"Don't—" I began, but Sidney was right side up again, walking toward her.

"Let's see," he said. "What outlet?"

He climbed the fence and looked at it, and then I could tell from his voice that he was worried.

"Darers go first!" he said.

"I did already. You can ask Berries."

"She did, and Hal said no one ought to do it again. He said—"

"It doesn't look very far," said Sidney, considering.

I climbed on the fence and yelled at them. "Hal *said*—you know he said it's too dangerous!"

In the cold silence we all sniffed and swiped at our dripping noses with our mittens. Sandra took her thumb

120

and held it to one nostril, and blew.

She looked at Sidney, just daring him to be as tough as she was. She said, "You better not do it. Your mother said to be careful, remember? Probably you're too little."

That did it. Sidney poised, rocked back, and ran at the jump. I held my breath, biting my frozen mitten.

He made it across. He fell forward, scrabbling for a hand hold. The ground was frozen hard and his mittens must have been stiff like mine. He slid down backwards, and we heard a sort of thump and a light spatter of gravel. Then silence.

I drew another breath—it had all only taken an instant—and yelled, "Sidney!"

No answer. I looked at Sandra, and we ran to the edge and looked down. We could barely make out the white blur of his face.

"We can go round and crawl through the culvert," she said.

"How'll we see?"

"I've got matches." She did, too. I bet her mother didn't know.

We pushed through the bushes to the far end of the culvert. It was a big pipe, at least three feet in diameter, with a shiny ribbon of ice at the bottom. Hardly any water was running out of the pond at this time of year.

121

Sandra lit a match. It made a warm circle of light, and the shadows beyond shot up, blacker than ever. The match went out.

I'll say this for Sandra—she went first. At the far end she lit another match so I could see my way to follow her. In the soft light, the walls of the pipe curved around me. I didn't want to come out. I didn't want to see what might have happened to Sidney.

"Come on, don't be afraid!" Sandra pulled me out beside her as the match went out, but she was scared too. We felt our way along the rock-lined trench between the pond dam and the pipe.

Sandra lit another match. Sidney was lying on his back, looking up. Blood ran out of his eyes and nose and mouth. The match went out.

Please God, make it not true, I said to myself. I didn't know blood could come out of a person's eyes.

Sandra was shaking. The next match broke off, unlit, and then she dropped the book. We patted the rocks with our hands till we found them again. I heard her draw a breath and hold it while she lit another.

The second look, somehow, was not quite as bad. Sidney moved his head and made a soft whimpering noise, and he became a person again. Sandra jumped up and started planning and organizing.

"There are only a couple of matches left," she said.

"We've got to save them. Take your coat off, and we'll put him on it and pull him through the culvert."

I was too numb to argue. I fumbled with the buttons and got the coat off and spread it on the ground.

"Pick up his feet!"

She grappled with his head and shoulders and got him onto the coat, and she pulled by the sleeves and collar, while I tried to push and steer. The bit of ice in the bottom of the culvert helped, and we slid him along fairly easily.

Outside the culvert we stopped. Sidney made a strange gurgling sound in his throat. Sandra straightened up hurriedly and said, "I better run for Mother. It's only about a mile—I'll go fast. Here, I'll leave you the last match."

"But . . ." My teeth chattered so I could hardly talk, and I couldn't think what to say anyway. I just knew I was scared to stay alone.

"You can put my jacket on. I'll be warm running." She put it round me and dashed off, and I knew she ran because she was scared to stay, even scareder than me.

I squatted and hunched up to try to keep warm. Sidney moaned and I said, "Please get better, Sidney, please get better."

I held the match in my stiff mitten, not daring to light it, because then I'd have nothing.

I I

All That Trouble

Long before I thought Sandra could have reached home for help, a car's headlights swept the pond and I heard Mrs. Graham's voice: "Sandra! Berries! Who-hoo!"

I scurried through the bushes, shouting and waving. She saw me and got out of the car. "What in the world are you doing down there? Why didn't you silly children get someone to give you a lift home?"

"Didn't Sandra find you?"

She looked at me crossly. "Sandra? Isn't she here?"

"She ran to get you. Sidney fell in . . . he's all bleeding . . . he's . . ."

"Fell in where? The ice is a foot thick."

I grabbed her by the sleeve and pulled her along to where Sidney was lying on the coat. The headlights threw a little light. She bent down and said, "Tch! Tch!" She shook his shoulder a little and said, "Sidney! Sidney, answer me!"

"Don't," I said. "He's hurt. He can't talk."

"Mmm." She stood up a minute and seemed to be thinking. She lit a match and looked at her watch and clucked her tongue again, with annoyance. Finally she said, "Well, come along. I'll have to take him to the hospital."

She lifted him up and got him into the car and we tore off into the darkness. Finally we turned in at the Samaritan Hospital, and Mrs. Graham drove around back to the ambulance entrance and jumped out.

Men in white coveralls came out pushing a stretcher, and they put Sidney on it. Mrs. Graham followed them back in. No one said anything to me. Still shivering, I pressed myself into the back corner of the seat, hugging my arms around me and trying not to think the thoughts that kept crawling around the corners of my mind.

I sat there, in sort of a daze, till the car door opened suddenly, and Mrs. Graham said, "You can come inside. We'll have to wait awhile."

She brought me a cup of cocoa out of a machine and said, "Now, tell me what happened."

I couldn't explain it all. I just said we'd been playing and doing tricks to keep warm, and Sidney tripped and fell. Then I asked her, "What happened to Hal? He said he'd be right back. Sandra said we had to wait for him."

"The car broke down. He had to call a garage to tow him, and he phoned me to come and get you."

"Oh." We sat, in our separate silences.

Suddenly Sidney's mother burst into the waiting room. She was crying, sobbing, and holding a handkerchief to her face. I had never seen a grown-up cry before, and I felt even more scared.

Her voice was high and shaky. "Where is he? Where's the doctor? What've they done with him?"

Mrs. Graham said, "You must try to be calm, Mrs. Fine. I'm sure everything will be all right. The doctors are with Sidney."

The words were comforting enough, but the way Mrs. Graham spoke I could see she didn't think Sidney's mother should be crying, right out loud in public.

Mrs. Fine caught the disapproval too, and she snapped, "Everything's *not* all right! They told me he's unconscious! You don't have to try to calm me down!"

She swung around and went to talk to the nurse at the desk, sniffing as she talked. The nurse patted her on the shoulder and said, "You can see him in just a minute, Mrs. Fine. As soon as the doctor comes out."

Mrs. Fine walked around the waiting room restlessly. She didn't seem to notice me at all. Suddenly she stopped and asked Mrs. Graham, "Who was with the children? Were they there alone?"

"Berries' older brother took them. Then he left for a bit, and his car broke down—"

She was interrupted by the doctor coming in, and he took Mrs. Fine by the arm and they started toward the corridor.

"Tell Sidney I'll come see him," I called.

"Mrs. Fine—I'll have to go home now. I'll phone you," Mrs. Graham called.

Neither of us got any answer. Sandra's mother stopped at the main desk as we were leaving and asked, "The little Fine boy, will . . . I mean, how is he?"

"He's still unconscious, ma'am. You'll have to call later for information."

Unconscious. Unconscious on television looked the same as dead, but of course that was only actors faking. How could you tell the difference, really?

As we drove home, I stared out ahead, half hypnotized by the headlights. That Sandra, I thought. Why did she always have it in for Sidney? Why didn't I stop him? I could have grabbed him. . . . I could have made them walk home. . . . It was no use, though, I hadn't. I wasn't the bossy kind. Sandra was. Like her mother.

The car stopped at our driveway. "Run along in, it's late," said Mrs. Graham. It was just her ordinary telling-everyone-what-to-do voice, not as if anything special had happened.

I plodded up the driveway, feeling as if it were maybe a driveway on the moon, not real. But there were Mavis and Jennifer in the kitchen, finishing supper.

Mavis said, "Goodness, Berries, you *are* late! Didn't Mrs. Graham pick you up? Hal said . . . well, never mind, run along and wash. Your dinner's waiting."

I stared at her and walked through the kitchen and living room to the stairs. Mom said, "Hello, dear," and Hal said, "About time!" I went up the stairs and into my room. I sat on the edge of my bed, but I couldn't seem to think at all. I heard Hal and Kite, playing cards downstairs, exchanging short remarks. Mavis called, "Berries! Where is that boy?" Hal slapped down his cards and said, "You won. I'll go see what's happened to Berries." Then there were his footsteps on the stairs. He came in and closed the door behind him.

"What's up, Berries? I went up and asked Sandra why you weren't home yet. She strung me some story about her mother taking you to the village, but I can always tell when she's lying. What's up?"

I knew if I tried to say anything, I'd cry. But I

couldn't just sit there. Finally I opened my mouth, and the sobs started pouring out, and I lay on the bed and choked. I didn't think I'd ever be able to stop. After a while Hal sat down on the end of the bed.

He tried to coax me. "Come on, Berries; it can't be that bad. Just tell me what it's all about."

There was nothing I could do to stop myself crying. Every time I tried to talk, I hiccuped. Finally, I told Hal more or less what had happened. I ended up, "He's unconscious. He can't talk or anything. He's probably going to die."

Hal said, "Being unconscious doesn't mean you're going to die. A kid in our school got kicked in the head and he was unconscious. It was a concussion. He was all right a few days later. Come on down. We'll get Mom to call the hospital and find out."

I shook my head. "I'm not coming down."

Hal went down, and I heard him talking to Mom and Dad for quite a while. I lay on the bed, and I may even have fallen asleep. Then Mom was sitting on the bed beside me, taking my shoes off. She whispered, "You mustn't worry, Berries. I called the hospital, and they said he was unconscious for a while, and now he's asleep. You go to sleep, too."

The next morning, Mom said she'd drive down to the hospital with me, so we could find out about Sidney.

129

The nurse at the main desk said he was doing as well as could be expected, which didn't seem to mean much. So we waited around. There was a man sitting by himself waiting too, and I thought it was Sidney's father. He didn't seem to know me, and I'd only met him a couple of times, so I wasn't sure.

Suddenly Sidney's mother came in through a door behind us. She didn't even see Mom and me; she went right over to the man, and it was Sidney's father. She said, "He's awake. Thank heaven! I haven't slept all night. I just sat beside him, waiting. He talked to me a little. He told me what happened."

They talked together quietly, and then he put his arm around her and said, "Come on, you'd better come home and get some rest. We'll come back later."

Before Mom could stop me, I went over and picked at her sleeve. "Mrs. Fine," I said, "is Sidney better? Can I see him?"

She pulled away, looking startled and angry. "No, of course not. He can't see anyone." Then her face softened a little and she said, "He'll be all right, but he has to lie very quiet."

She didn't pay any more attention to me. She just took Mr. Fine's arm and they started toward the door. At the door, my mother stopped her and said, "Mrs. Fine, I'm so sorry about the accident. I do hope he'll be all right in a few days. If there's anything I could do to help . . ."

Sidney's mother just looked at her, and then she walked on out the door. Mom and I followed and walked toward our car in the parking lot. I watched Sidney's mother and father go to their car. Outside it they stopped and seemed to be having an argument. I heard Mrs. Fine's voice rise, and I remembered how Sidney said she sometimes got really upset. Mr. Fine was holding her arm, but she pulled away from him. She looked right at Mom and came toward us.

Mom hadn't seen her coming, and she swung around in surprise when Mrs. Fine's voice hit her. "I'll tell you what you could have done, but it's too late now. You could watch the children, instead of sending them out alone! That Sandra needs to be watched; she's vicious, that's what she is!"

Mom stammered, "Mrs. Fine, I'm terribly sorry . . . my older son was with them. Then his car broke down. . . ."

"Oh, there's always an excuse, when it's too late! I know. It was just too much trouble. So forget it—you don't have to bother about my Sidney now."

She had turned and gone back to her car before Mom or I could say anything. Mom didn't say anything to me either. She looked a million miles away, and she

131

drove faster than usual going home. Hal and Kite were still eating breakfast in the kitchen. Mom went right past them and up to her hideaway.

I slammed the kitchen cupboard. It popped open and I slammed it again. I don't mind if Mom hides when we're all being noisy, but this time I wished she'd talk to me.

"Sidney's better, isn't he?" Hal asked.

"Ye-es. I couldn't see him though. We saw his mother. She was—I don't know. Of course she'd be worried. But she was angry too."

"At you?"

"Well, no, at Mom mostly. And she said Sandra's vicious—what's that mean? She thinks we don't care that Sidney got hurt, or something. Doesn't she know he's my best friend?"

Hal looked miserable. "It *was* my fault. We should never have left you alone at the pond. I got so sick of Sandra and . . ."

"But there were plenty of people there," Kite said. "It really was an accident, the way everything happened."

"Why can't Sidney's mother understand that it was an accident? Why is she so angry?"

Hal frowned. "The other thing is . . . you know the way Sandra and her family talk about Jewish people. So does . . . well, so do a lot of people. I suppose Sidney's mother knows how some people feel. Then an accident happens, and she thinks, 'They don't care what happens to us; they never liked us anyway.' So she blows up."

"Probably she'll calm down later. After all, she was tired and worried. She may have been up all night." Kite said that, and I tried to hope she was right.

I 2

Mothers

I waited a few days, and then I began nagging at Mom. "Call up Sidney's mother, can't you? Call her."

"M-mm . . . I'll call the hospital," Mom said. So she did, and they said he was out of danger, and he was sitting up in bed.

"Great. Then I can go see him, can't I?"

"You'll have to wait till we hear from Mrs. Fine."

"Well, *call* her then!"

But she wouldn't. She said we'd better wait. Finally one day when Mom was out, I called the Fines' house. Mrs. Fine answered. She didn't sound as cheery as usual when I said it was me. I asked if I could go see Sidney at the hospital.

"He can't have any visitors except the family," she said.

"I'd be careful," I said. "I'd just talk to him; I wouldn't jump around."

"I'm sorry, Berries. No visitors." And that was that.

Sandra and I fooled around outside after school sometimes, but it was too cold and it got dark too early to do anything much.

"You didn't tell anyone I dared Sidney to jump, did you?" Sandra asked me. We were waiting for Spooky to finish her dinner.

"I don't think so. What difference does it make?"

"Well—don't tell anyone."

I grunted. I wasn't interested in Sandra; I just wanted to know when I could see Sidney again.

The next Sunday suddenly Mrs. Graham and Sandra appeared at our house. It was the first time Sandra's mother had been in our house. She found Mom in the living room reading the papers, and Hal was doing his homework. Dad was outdoors. Sandra stopped with me in the kitchen to look at a model I was building, and I think her mother forgot she was there.

Right off she said to Mom, "I've got to talk to you about this Mrs. Fine."

Mom sounded puzzled. "Sidney's mother?"

"Yes. You know, I'd really been expecting she might phone and thank me for taking care of Sidney that night. After all, I hung around the hospital quite a while. I had company coming and no dinner cooked and . . . well, that's not the point.

"Anyway, I got thinking in church this morning, and I decided I should call her up, just to inquire about the little boy, you know, just to be pleasant.

"Well, I practically got blown off the phone! Thanks, indeed! I certainly didn't get any thanks! She practically blames the whole accident on me. She says Sandra is vicious, she's always persecuted her little boy. That was her exact word—*persecuted*. So ridiculous!"

Sandra pricked up her ears and edged toward the living room, when she heard her mother talking about her.

My mother said, "The accident certainly wasn't *your* fault. Sidney was visiting us."

"She practically accused Sandra of pushing him!"

This was too much for Sandra. She said, "I didn't push him! I never did! He's lying!"

Hal looked up. "Well, you were *there*. You knew how dangerous that culvert was—remember, I told you last year. Why didn't you tell him to keep away from it?"

Sandra pouted and muttered to me, "It's none of his business."

Her mother took over. "Well, that's beside the point. Sandra's not an adult. She's not supposed to take *care* of him."

Sandra stuck her tongue out a little at Hal and looked smug. I hadn't meant to say anything, but suddenly I couldn't stand the look on her face. Her and her mother—everything they did had to be right. I yelled, "She dared him to jump that culvert! She made him do it!"

The grown-ups all stopped and stared at me.

"Come now, Berries, don't invent," said Sandra's mother.

I had to go on. "She said it was easy to jump that culvert. She told him she'd done it. Then she kept needling him—saying she guessed he was too little, or he was a sissy. Just because she doesn't want him to be my friend."

"I hate you, you little sissy tattletale!" Sandra hissed at me. Then she stuck her jaw out and said to the others, "I didn't *make* him do anything! I said I'd done it, and it was easy. It is. I should think Sidney could have done it, too."

I shouted, "Well, he tried—he's not a sissy! Anyway, you wanted him to fall. I know you did. Now I can't play with him, and it's all your fault! I hope they come and put you in prison!"

"All right, Berries, that's enough shouting," said

137

Mrs. Graham. "Children dare each other all the time. Of course, some of these . . . uh . . . children are overprotected. Babied. It's unfortunate, of course. Sidney just wasn't as able. There's no need for all this fuss. He's out of danger now."

There she was, with her big, sure steamroller face, writing the whole thing off, nothing worth fussing about. After talking to *her,* Sidney's mother is probably so angry she'll never let him come here again, I thought. Then I stopped thinking and put my head down and charged. Mrs. Graham didn't expect it. My head hit her amidships, and I flailed with both arms and kicked at her shins.

Finally I guess Hal got ahold of me. I remember him putting me over his shoulder and carrying me upstairs. He dropped me on my bed, where I went on kicking and pounding.

Hours later, I came downstairs, and I supposed I'd really get punished or scolded. But no one said anything; they treated me sort of gingerly, as if I might explode.

I didn't really see Mrs. Graham to talk to again after that. A few days later, I saw Sandra down at the far end of our yard, talking to Spooky and looking sideways at our house. I went out.

"Mom says . . . " Sandra began as she always did,

quoting the oracle. But this time she sounded apologetic; she wanted me to know it wasn't her idea. "She says I'm not supposed to go in your house."

"I wouldn't go in your house if you paid me! I hate your mother."

"Well, I hate my mother trying to tell me who I should play with and who's going to be my friend. I can make up my own mind. She doesn't need to be so bossy. Come on, let's get up in the treehouse. It's more fun with no grown-ups around, anyway."

Up in the treehouse she went on, "You know, I didn't want Sidney to fall and get hurt. I never did. I didn't think he'd ever jump; I thought he'd chicken out. Still, I suppose it was sort of my fault, so we ought to do something to make up. Let's buy get-well cards with our own money and send Sidney one every day."

"I spent all my money at Christmas," I objected. "Besides, it wasn't *my* fault."

"Well, I'll get the cards, and you can borrow stamps from your mother."

"I'd rather figure out how I can get to see Sidney."

"Well, if we send a lot of cards, his mother will know we're worrying about him. Then you can call her, and she'll let you go see him."

I figured it was worth trying, so we spent several afternoons up in the treehouse, blowing on our fingers,

139

writing and addressing cards. Your fingers get so cold they really hurt, and I thought Mrs. Fine couldn't help being impressed. We sent off a whole bunch; then I waited a few days and asked Mom to phone Mrs. Fine. She didn't want to, so I tackled Dad.

"I can find out how he is from the hospital," he said.

"But I want to know if I can *see* him. You have to ask his mother."

"Well, all right." He got on the phone, and he talked in his office voice, sort of extra polite and jovial. "My little boy would certainly like to say hello to Sidney. We're all so relieved he's better. Do you suppose Berries could put his head in, just to say Hello?"

"I don't just want to say Hello, I want to *talk*," I muttered.

"Oh, I see. Well, of course." The cheery, chummy sound had definitely gone out of Dad's voice. "I'll call again in a week or two. Good-bye."

"A *week* or two! Why do I have to wait so long, if he's better?"

"Berries, I'm sorry," Dad said. "But she didn't sound as if she even wanted to talk to me. She's still pretty upset."

"Well, when's she going to get better? Sidney's better. Why isn't she?"

140

"I don't know," Dad said, and he sat down and picked up his newspaper.

My only pipeline for information about Sidney was Hal, because Sidney's older brother, Marty, was in high school with him. After a couple of weeks, Hal told me Sidney had gone home from the hospital.

Great, I thought. Now I can talk to him on the phone at least. I waited till no one was in the kitchen who might yell at me to quit tying up the phone. Then I called. I got Mrs. Fine.

"Hello, Mrs. Fine; it's me, Berries. Hal told me Sidney was home. Can I speak to him?"

"Uh . . . uh . . . just a minute please." She put the phone down, and I thought she'd gone to get him. She came back herself and said, "I'm sorry, he's asleep."

"Asleep! It's only five o'clock!"

"Yes. Well, he's asleep."

In the back of my head I knew it wasn't true, but I just said, "Can I call him later? He'll be awake later, won't he?"

There was too long a pause. Then she said, "I'd rather you didn't anymore. I'm sorry, I have to go now. Good-bye."

I heard the phone click. I stared at the empty receiver in my hand, and finally I hung it up. She can't mean it, I thought. She can't mean I shouldn't call him ever. But how can a kid argue with a grown-up, when she sounds all cold and distant like that? I thought of calling again several other times, but I didn't dare. I began to see how Mom felt about making phone calls. When you think someone doesn't like you, you don't dare.

Anyway, I figured, if he's home now, pretty soon he'll be back in school. I kept pestering Hal to find out from Marty when Sidney was coming back.

In February Hal came home one afternoon and saw me outside with Spooky. After a little hacking around about the weather and stuff, he said, "I talked to Marty Fine some more today."

"Well, what'd he say?"

"He said Sidney has been transferred. He said he's going to Indian Road school now."

"They can't do that—he's in our school!"

"Marty said his mother got him transferred. He says she feels safer having him there, where a lot of their friends go."

"But . . . we . . ." I tried to object, but I could feel my voice choking up, and I knew there was nothing I could do. Stinking grown-ups—they shoved everyone around; they didn't even care Sidney was my best friend.

I ran away, and Spooky chased after me, nipping at my blue jeans. At the foot of the treehouse, I grabbed her and carried her up with me. It was the first time I'd taken Spooky in the treehouse, and she was scared. She shook all over. I hugged her tight and snuffled into her fur.

After a while I got cold and Spooky was still trembling, so we got down. I kicked rocks around the yard and said to myself, I'll show them. They're not going to get away with it. I'll find a way to see Sidney.

13

Bicycle

At first I couldn't really believe it. I kept thinking I'd run into Sidney somewhere, like at the store or the post office, and his mother would say, "Hello there, Berries," and everything would be the way it had been. I couldn't believe someone's parents could really stop him seeing his friends. I called him up once, but his mother answered the phone. I got scared and just hung up without saying a word.

At school I still hung around with Jack, and he helped me with my arithmetic, but it wasn't the same. Without Sidney, Jack and I just didn't seem to stick together.

Sandra still came around, especially when she was

mad at her mother. You'd think after Mrs. Graham tried to cover up for her about daring Sidney to jump, she'd imitate her mother even more. But it worked just the other way. She seemed annoyed at everything her mother told her to do now. She was getting a lot bigger too, and she made a bunch of new friends at school.

"Susan and Bunkie are coming to play Saturday," she told me once. She added with satisfaction, "My mother doesn't like either of them."

February and March crawled by. I missed Sidney at school and around home too—we'd always visited each other at least a couple of times a week. I was left to hang around with Jennifer and Spooky, and neither of them would do what I told them. Mavis poked me along to go with them on their walks. On Mavis's days off we didn't usually bother to go out, and Jennifer had her thumb in her mouth most of the day. When I got home from school, we flopped in front of television. Mostly we were still there when Dad came home, and Jen was so hypnotized by TV she'd hardly take her thumb out to say hello to him.

Along in April, when the weather improved, Dad started yelling. "Why're you two always lying in here like slugs? Get out and *do* something!"

"Nothing to do." I scowled.

"Ride your bike."

"It's no good. It's too small."

"Start digging a garden."

"I don't feel like a garden."

"You could just feel like a *boy*, for a start," he said, but I didn't.

The next Saturday, after breakfast, Dad said, "Come on, Berries, we're going to Oxford."

"Oh. What for?"

"Business."

I frowned, because it had got to be a habit, but I was glad to go along. We went to the big Sears Roebuck at the shopping center, and Dad walked right to the back where the garden equipment and bicycles were. Seeds and fertilizer, I thought. Dad cast his eye down the row of bicycles and said, "O.K., no six-speed gear shifts, no electric floodlight, no sidecar—just pick out a good serviceable bike. Fifty bucks or under."

"Me?"

"You."

"You mean, for me? For my own?"

"Unless you've got a rat in your pocket."

I walked up and down the row of bikes in a daze. Not having had it in my mind, it took me quite a while to decide. I finally narrowed it down to a gold-colored three-speed English bike, and a glossy black one with no gears or hand brakes—but it did have a pump, headlight, horn, and baggage rack—all for $48.99. The gold one was $45.99. I yearned over the gears and hand brakes awhile, but I remembered Jack's gears were always out of order, and I really liked the black one best.

We wheeled it out and put it in the car, and I squeezed in back right beside it. About halfway home I remembered to say, "Gee, thanks, Dad."

"That's all right," he said. "But your brother's going to blow a fuse."

He did, too. Hal had a bike, but it was an old crock, and it hadn't been as good as mine when it was new. He squawked, "For crying out loud, it's not even his birthday! How does he rate this?"

"He needs it," said Dad.

"What line did you hand him?" Hal asked me.

"Nothing. I never even asked him. He just did it." I thought a bit and added, "Now I've got it, I guess I'll get me a paper route or something."

Mom glared at Dad. "Are you going to let him ride that thing on the main road?"

"Yes," said Dad. "Come on, Berries, I'll take Hal's bike and show you where to ride and how to watch traffic."

We rolled down the hill, leaving Mom and Hal glaring.

After that it was as if I'd moved to a different planet. I'd never noticed much about the roads we drove on around Olcott Corners. Now I learned which ones had puddles like lakes to ride through after a rain; which ones had gravel that could skid you over on your elbow; which ones had barking dogs; and the one that had a real biting dog, so you didn't go that way.

Sometimes I rode with Jack, or some other kid from school, or Sandra, but she had a slow old balloon tire job. Pretty often I went exploring alone.

Mom fretted her head off at first. She made me tell Mavis whose house I was going to and telephone when I got there and when I was starting back. After I survived the first month, she began to relax.

I was away down on the south side of town one day, sort of hunting for a place to go fishing. I was keeping to the back roads, because Spooky had followed me, and she wasn't too smart about traffic. I came around a corner toward an overgrown field, and there was a kid sitting on the fence. Spooky trotted past, running slantwise and nose down, the way she does. Suddenly she stopped and ran back to the kid and started jumping all over him. It was Sidney.

"Look, she remembers me!" he crowed.

"Sure, she'd always know you." We looked at each other, and I said, "How come you're sitting on the fence reading?"

"If I sit and read at home, Mom comes and asks me if I feel all right. She's always fussing at me."

148

"Yeah, my mom is always fussing about where I'm going on the bike. Pretty neat bike, huh?"

"Yeah." Sidney looked it all over and ran his hand over the glossy fender. "They won't even let me ride Marty's big bike. Fuss, fuss, fuss. Let me try it."

"Go ahead."

There was a big boulder beside the road that he could get on from. He started off, wobbling a good deal, with Spooky barking madly, but by the time he came back he was going straight as an arrow, and he swung his leg over to jump off as if he'd been doing it always.

"Wow!" he said. He wheeled it up to the boulder and went off again. By the third try he could swing his leg over to get on. "Can you come down here often so I can ride?"

"Sure, I could come most any time after school, or weekends."

A car went by, and a kid from my school leaned out and waved. Sidney and I looked at each other, and simultaneously we swung over the fence and crouched behind it.

"We got to watch out," Sidney said. "They'd make trouble if they found me here."

"Yeah, you're not supposed to ride the bike. Or anything."

We both knew what I meant. Sidney said, "We got to make a plan. So they don't know you're hanging around here."

I looked behind us into the field. It was thick with bushes and brambles. I lifted my bike over the fence and laid it down out of sight. "Come on," I said, and headed into the thickest bushes.

We pushed in quite a ways, until we found a really dense thicket. I said, "There. We can make a hideout in the middle."

Sidney started to plunge in, but I made him come around to the back side, so our entrance wouldn't show. Also we tunneled in through the brambles on hands and knees, so the bushes weren't broken at eye level. In the middle of the thicket we trampled down bushes to round out a little room.

Sidney grinned. "This is neat! Look, the bushes even make a roof over us, almost."

We squatted down to plot. I said, "We'll have to set a day to meet, so I won't be hanging around these roads too often. Saturday?"

Sidney frowned. "Trouble is, sometimes we all go somewhere Saturday, and I wouldn't be able to let you know. Wednesday. Wednesday my mother plays bridge, and Marty doesn't bother where I go."

"Wednesday'd be great. My mother goes to the A & P then."

150

We settled on Wednesdays. It didn't seem like an awful lot of time, but we figured maybe we could work in an extra day sometimes, too. After that we sat and talked. He said Indian Road school was lousy, he wasn't even the brightest kid in the class, and there were no overhead bars to swing from in the playground. I told him I didn't see as much of Sandra anymore; she was getting too old, I guess.

There was a short silence, and I said, "Did you get all the cards me and Sandra sent to the hospital? We almost froze writing them in the treehouse."

"No, I didn't get any," he said. There was a longer silence. That was all we ever said about the accident.

Sidney was the first to notice it was getting dark. "Come on, we got to get home. We don't want to do anything to make them suspicious. Everything's got to seem just as usual."

For the rest of that spring my life revolved around Wednesdays. For the first three in a row, it rained. We stuck it out, squatting and shivering in our raincoats, with Spooky looking disgusted with us. The third time, I brought a tarp to put over the bushes, and that was better, but it showed.

When the weather improved, I began bringing tools and wire and boards to fix up the hideout on the inside. One Wednesday Sandra saw me setting off with a load of stuff, and she asked where I was going.

151

"Just riding. I got to leave some stuff off with a kid."

"Huh." Sandra had a suspicious nature, so of course she kept an eye out until she saw me going off with another load—old window screens this time.

"You sure take that kid a lot of good stuff," she said.

"Uh, yeah," I mumbled.

"Must be a pretty fancy hideout."

"I never said it was a hideout!" I shot back.

Sandra laughed in my face and said, "Sucker. You sure bit on that one."

"Listen, don't you go telling anyone." I was worried. My dad had begun shouting about the tools already.

Sandra considered, in a queenly manner. "I won't tell anyone, if you let me know who you're building the hideout with."

"I can't."

"Then it's someone you're not supposed to see."

"It's not . . . it's not anyone you know!" I fumbled.

"Liar! I bet it's Sidney," she said scornfully.

I couldn't say anything, and Sandra turned away. I ran and grabbed her shoulder. "Sandra, if you ever tell, I'll . . . I mean it this time; I'll do something awful!"

"All right," she said, sounding almost bored. "I won't."

I didn't tell Sidney about this, because he worried an awful lot anyway. We went on building, and we really had a fancy hideout, roofed in and screened against mosquitoes. With all the building, it was late before we started home. I remembered to take the tools home—all that I could find anyway—so no one would get on my trail.

I was just starting to straddle the fence, when a car went by. Not just *any* car—our car, with Hal driving. I ducked fast and prayed that he hadn't recognized me. He didn't stop.

"What's up?" said Sidney.

"A car went by. I thought it was someone I knew."

He frowned. "We better leave separately. You go ahead. I'll stay hidden till you're out of sight."

"O.K. So long. N.W." That was our code for "Next Wednesday."

"So long. N.W."

Hal saw me stashing the tools away in the garage when I got back, and he didn't say anything. I guessed he hadn't recognized the bike. Mom asked why I was so late, and I said I was building a treehouse with a kid.

"I called Jack, and he said you'd gone right home from school."

"It wasn't Jack, it was Sandy." I didn't know anyone named Sandy.

"You'd better give me his phone number."

"O.K."

I banked on Mom forgetting about this after supper, which she did. Sidney and I continued to meet Wednesdays, taking care to arrive and depart separately.

Late in May we found a little brook about a half mile back into the woods. We worked late one afternoon damming it up to make a swimming hole. By the time we could get in, the sun had gone down. It was cold, and we realized it must be late. Sidney always kept track of the time, but he'd had his watch off on account of the water. We hot-footed it for the road.

Sidney was ahead and scrambled over the fence. "Oh, there you are!" a voice said. It was Hal's voice.

Then my dad said, "Is Berries with you?"

I could feel Sidney gulping, and then he said in a tight, flat voice, "Berries? No, I haven't seen him."

That kid certainly wasn't a practiced liar. Hal said, "Come on, I saw him here last week. Of course he's with you."

I came out then. I burst out, "Gee, Dad, we found the neatest brook! It's way back there in the woods. I bet no one ever found it before, and it took us all afternoon to build a dam for a swimming hole. Then Sidney lost his watch, and we spent an hour hunting for it, and—well, that's how it got so late. We didn't mean to."

"Well, your mother's having a fit. She thought you'd fallen down the gorge. Jump in. Sidney, can we give you a ride home?"

Sidney gulped again. "Oh, no! It's not that far away. I'll walk."

We almost got away. We probably missed by the amount of time it took me to get the bike in the car. Dad had just started the car when another car came toward us, and the driver stopped right beside Dad. Sidney was on the grass behind our car, momentarily hidden from the other driver, who was his father.

Mr. Fine looked startled to see Dad. Dad said, "Hello, Mr. Fine. These kids sure lead us quite a chase, don't they? Berries said they were just building a swimming pool."

Mr. Fine looked puzzled and at the same time he spotted Sidney. He pulled his car off to the other side of the road. "You get in that car!" he said to Sidney.

He walked across to Dad and said, "Could I have a word with you?"

"Why, sure," Dad said. Finally he realized Mr. Fine wanted him to get out of the car, and the two of them walked a little way down the road, where we couldn't hear them. I peered over at Sidney in his car, and he beckoned to me. I went around to the far side of his car.

"You got your pocketknife?"

I felt my pockets. "Uh, yeah. What for?"

"Give it here."

"Listen, don't . . ." I trailed off, watching him open the blade, stick out his left index finger, and quickly cut it.

He handed me the knife and said, "Hurry. Cut yours."

It's not so easy to cut your own finger on purpose. First try I failed and felt like a chicken. I drew blood the second time.

Sidney grabbed my hand and rubbed our two bleeding fingers together. "There. Whatever they do, we're blood brothers now. Promise."

"Uh—O.K. I promise."

Sidney's father came to get in the car. He looked at me, and I faded off. They drove away. Sidney didn't turn around or wave.

Hal was in the back seat of our car reading the Oxford paper. Dad looked sort of grim. He got rolling toward home, and finally he cleared his throat and said, "Mr. Fine doesn't want you to meet Sidney anymore."

"I know."

Dad looked surprised. We drove along for a few more minutes, and then he cleared his throat again.

"He said Mrs. Fine is very nervous, especially since the accident last winter. If she knew Sidney was playing with you, she'd get all upset. She might really get sick."

I grunted.

Dad frowned and drove along without speaking till we got home. Hal got out and wandered up the driveway still looking at the paper. Dad said, "Listen, Berries, I'm sorry it's like this, but will you promise me not to meet Sidney anymore? Because I pretty much promised Mr. Fine."

"So you already promised." I could feel my lip sticking out, the way it does when I think someone's pushing me into a corner.

"Well, it's just . . . I mean, I don't want to tell Mom she's got to *watch* you every minute. Let's just make a gentlemen's agreement."

I sat staring at the floor and blinking my eyes, because I had that awful feeling again.

"O.K.?" Dad asked.

I jumped out of the car and shouted at him over my shoulder. "You're my father, you can just *tell* me! You don't have to pretend it's any old gentlemen's agreement! It's not!"

I left him sitting there.

14

The Other Goodmans

There I was again, without Sidney. Even if I couldn't meet him at the hideout—I knew his father wouldn't let him go there anymore—I didn't see why I couldn't just happen to run into him somewhere else. I rode my bike around all the roads near Olcott Acres day after day. But I never saw him.

There was some excitement around home. We'd been out in Olcott for just two years that June, and our lease was due to run out. The FOR SALE sign had been up on our driveway since early in the spring. Dad asked Mom what she was planning to do if someone came along and bought the place out from under us. Mom looked pleased. She said she could always find something. She began working harder on real estate, so as to keep an eye on the possibilities, and because she still hoped to make our fortune.

The chances of our house being sold in a hurry weren't great. Hal and I used to lay bets on the probable expression on people's faces—alarm, embarrassment, or disapproval—when they discovered the bathroom up the kitchen stairs. The house's roof and cellar still leaked, the paint was two years worse than it had been, and the muddle of Goodman living all over the place didn't help the viewer's first impression. Miss Curmudgeon in the real estate office thought we left things in a mess on purpose so the house wouldn't be sold, but it was really just our normal way of life.

When I thought about the long dull summer ahead, I got pretty gloomy. I hoped we'd sell the house and move somewhere else. There isn't any use living in a place where you don't have a best friend.

Hal was going away—he had a camp job lined up so he could earn money before going to college. Sandra was getting packed off to a camp in Maine. The year before she'd been begging to go to camp, but now she didn't want to go. She said her mother was just trying to stop her playing with me, and with Susan and Bunkie.

Dad was working longer hours than he used to. He had got promoted, and they were making a lot of changes in the magazine, and he had to work on Saturdays even. Mom was steamed up about another real estate ad she'd seen in the Oxford paper. A European count with lots of money and grandchildren wanted to sell his elegant city penthouse apartment, which his grandchildren must have been wrecking, and buy a spacious country estate.

Mom phoned him and found out his penthouse was in our old neighborhood in New York. Mom got homesick talking about all the old landmarks and talked on the phone for half an hour, before finally pinning him down to come out and look at estates. He came, and he had wavy white hair and he bowed over Mom's hand. She just loved it. She also loved the idea of selling him a big country estate.

I actually got stuck baby-sitting for Jennifer a couple of times when Mavis was on vacation. The first time, Jen made lipstick pictures all over the kitchen cabinets, and the next time she ate all the sugar in the bowl, except that half of it spilled on the floor. After that Mom took Jennifer along if Hal wasn't home.

She was all set for a tour of estates with the count one Saturday in June. Hal had to go to graduation rehearsal and Dad was working, so Mom took Jen and left me home alone, after a prolonged lecture about not lighting any fires or swimming in the pond. Anybody'd have thought I was still six years old.

I started cleaning out my closet, because sometimes there were pretty good things back in there that I'd forgotten I ever had. I got all the junk out, but there really wasn't much interesting, so I went down to fix something to eat.

I was experimenting with orange juice concentrate on toast (it melts and the toast gets soggy) when a kid peered in the kitchen door and called to me. Still not quite recognizing him, I opened the door.

"Hiya, Cousin Berries," he said. "Surprise, surprise!"

"Gee—Cousin Iz! How'd you get out here?" It was Izzy Goodman, a kid that used to be in my school in New York. He was about two years older than me, but he lived near us and we sometimes walked home together. On account of having the same last name, we used to call each other "cousin" as a joke.

He said, "Mom and Dad are down in the car. They've got this bug about living in the suburbs, now that we've got a new baby, so we came out to look at houses. I remembered Irvy said your mother sold real estate, so we looked her up in the phone book."

I tried to think fast. Mom would hate to lose a customer, but I wasn't sure where I could reach her. Finally I said, "Let's go down and tell your parents to come in, and I'll call the office and see if they know where Mom is."

161

We went down, and Izzy's mother said she would like to come in because she wanted to heat a bottle for the baby.

"Shall I get out the rest of the picnic stuff, Mom?" Izzy asked, sort of extra loud, and his mother looked embarrassed.

"That'd be great," I said. "Mom won't mind. I'm here alone, and I was just trying to figure out what to eat for lunch. Maybe by the time we eat, Mom'll be back anyway."

I helped Izzy carry the picnic stuff up, and boy, did they ever bring food! When *we* have a picnic, it's just peanut butter sandwiches or hot dogs, but they had all kinds of cold meat and cheese and pickles and onion rolls and fruit, not to mention six kinds of soda.

Mrs. Goodman fed the baby and put her to sleep in Jennifer's crib, and then she spread the picnic on the outdoor table. It was really a banquet.

I was finished eating and wondering about opening a third bottle of soda, when Mr. Goodman said, "I see you've got your own house up for sale. Where are you moving?"

"Oh, it's not our house—we just rent it. I don't think anyone'll ever buy, so we probably won't move."

"H-mm, pretty nice house. Nice yard, too," Mr. Goodman said. He got up and strolled around, looking at the pond and the house from different angles.

162

To be polite, I said, "We can look through the house, if you want."

"Fine," he said. "Come along, Betty."

Mrs. Goodman said she thought they ought to wait for Mom.

"Mom won't mind," I said. "Anyone can look at our house. It's always pretty messy anyway."

I showed them all around, and Mr. Goodman certainly paid a whole lot more attention than my dad ever had. We came back downstairs, and he said, "You're sure the house is for sale?"

"Oh, yes, quite a few people have looked at it. I don't think it's very expensive, because Mom said she wouldn't get a very good commission if she sold it. I could phone Miss Cur—Miss Carmichael down at the office. She knows all about it, and she might know where Mom is."

"Hey, Dad!" Izzy interrupted. "You might really buy this house?"

"Well, we can find out," said Mr. Goodman.

"Yippee!" shouted Iz.

I dialed the office and Miss Curmudgeon answered in her sugary voice: "Corner Real Estate!"

"This is Berries," I said. "My mother is out with that count, and some friends from the city came by to look at houses. Do you know where I could reach Mom?"

163

"No, dear, she hasn't phoned. What kind of house do your friends want?"

"Well, they like this one. Ours."

"How exciting, dear! Would they like to come down and talk to me?"

"I guess so." (I hate being called "dear.")

"Just send them down, dear. What's their name?"

"Goodman."

"Oh, your *cousins!* How nice. Maybe the house will stay right in the family! You send them down, and I'll tell your mother if she telephones. 'Bye, dear."

" 'Bye."

The Goodmans' baby was still asleep, so Mr. Goodman said he would go down and talk to Miss Carmichael about our house, and then perhaps they would drive around and look at some other houses.

"Can I go with you, Dad, can I?" Izzy jumped up and down.

Mr. Goodman looked at his bare feet and pants muddy from the pond, and he said, "No."

"Aw, gee, I'll probably never see you buy a house again," Izzy moped.

I said, "Never mind. I haven't shown you the really good things about this one yet. Like the treehouse."

Izzy perked right up, and by the time we had climbed up in the treehouse he was buzzing away, describing all the things he would do when it was *his* treehouse. I began to feel not so good. I began to think it was a pretty good house, with the pond and treehouse and everything. Then I heard Sandra calling from down below—she always came snooping around if I had a new friend over.

Iz looked down and said, "Who're you?"

"Who're you, yourself?" said Sandra.

"I just might be the new owner of this treehouse," Izzy announced, as Sandra climbed up.

She looked at him with more interest, but still rather suspicious. She asked him if he knew any secret codes, and he said of course he did. Then she asked if he had a fielder's glove, and he said he didn't but he had a new spinning rod, and he could bowl over a hundred.

"Gee," said Sandra. "I never bowled."

"It's neat. My father would take you, any time I asked him."

"When are you moving in?" Sandra asked.

I was getting pretty sick of this conversation. I said, "Listen, they don't even *know* yet. They might not *ever* buy it. If they do, we're going to get a house at the shore, with a boat and a kennel where Spooky can have puppies."

"You're just making that up," Sandra said scornfully. "Come on, let's show Izzy the tunnel back of the garage!"

She climbed down, with Izzy right behind her, and

she was telling him all the trick things about our garage and cellar before I could even catch up with them. It was like she was leading the guided tour.

Mr. Goodman came back with Miss Curmudgeon as we were crawling out of the tunnel. Miss Curmudgeon looked at our dirty knees and faces as if we were cute, and she said, "Berries, dear, your mother is certainly going to be proud of you! Just imagine, another real estate salesman in the family."

"Huh?" I sneezed some dirt out of my nose.

"I think your cousins are really going to buy your house," said Miss Curmudgeon. "Mr. Goodman said you showed him around, just as if you were a real agent."

Mr. Goodman looked puzzled by the "cousin" talk, but we were all interrupted at that point by Mom driving up and spraying out gravel as she jammed on the brakes.

"I did it! I really did it!" she shouted and jumped out and practically danced on the lawn. "I sold the count old man Griffin's hundred thousand dollar estate!"

Miss Curmudgeon's mouth hung open. She was really envious. Mom finally stopped dancing and noticed the Goodmans. "Why, hello! I was so excited I didn't even see you at first!"

Miss Curmudgeon was determined not to be

pushed entirely out of the limelight, and she grabbed me by the elbow and planted us in front of Mom. "Berries and I have news for you too! He's following right in your footsteps. He's shown your house to your cousins, and they expect to buy it. Now, isn't *that* a surprise?"

It seemed rather more than a surprise to Mom. She looked about to faint.

Mr. and Mrs. Goodman both looked embarrassed and they started speaking at once: "We're not really cousins; it's just the . . ." said Mr. Goodman.

"There! I knew we should have waited for you," said Mrs. Goodman to Mom. "You mustn't be upset. Nothing's settled at all yet. If we do buy, we're in no hurry to move in."

"Oh, it's perfectly . . . I don't mind . . . I love moving . . ." Mom babbled along as if she had no control over the words, but she stopped when she saw Dad and Hal walk up the drive. Someone must have given them a ride from the village.

"Boy, what is this, a convention?" Dad boomed. He shook hands all around and took Mrs. Goodman by the arm. "Well, come on up and sit down! We don't all have to stand around down here. How about some refreshment, Amy?"

The parade struggled up to the lawn chairs, with Dad bubbling along hospitably and no one else saying much. Mom wasn't making any move toward refreshments, so Izzy and I went and brought out the three remaining sodas.

"I think I'll just leave you all to celebrate," said Miss Curmudgeon, not looking very enthusiastic about soda. "I really must be getting back to the office. Perhaps Hal could drive me?"

They went off, and Dad offered their own sodas to the Goodmans, but they said they really must be going too.

"Why, I thought you just came," said Dad. "Why don't you stay for dinner?"

What an optimist—he really thought we might have that much food in the house!

Izzy interrupted: "Hey, Mr. Goodman, you know what?"

"That's what!" Dad answered automatically.

"No, seriously—we might buy this house. I like it and Mom and Dad like it too."

"And if they buy it, I ought to get the commission," I said. "I showed them all around and I called Miss Curmudgeon for them. Mom sold old Griffin's house to the count, so she'll get the commission on that."

Dad looked slowly from me to Mom to the Goodmans and he nodded. "So that's what the convention was all about."

Mr. Goodman spoke up. "Of course, nothing's

168

settled. The owner was out of town today. I gave Miss Carmichael a check as an option to buy, but nothing's going to happen in a hurry."

"Uh, no," said Dad, and he moved over and put an arm around Mom.

After a while the Goodmans gathered up their picnic baskets and baby and drove off, with Iz hanging out the window yelling, "So long, cousin!"

Hal came back, and I couldn't figure out why we were all just standing there still, with Mom and Dad staring off into space.

"Well," Mom said, "this is the end."

Dad tried to look innocent and confused, the way he does when he's forgotten to pick up the laundry.

Then Mom started laughing, and she laughed so hard she had to sit down and wipe her eyes. Dad and Hal looked worried.

"Well, it's funny," Mom finally gasped. "Here I've pulled off the real estate sale of my dreams, and now I'll be run out of town!"

"Oh, now, Amy, nothing's settled. Come on, let's go in and you tell me all about this deal with the count." He was faking—I can always tell. He just wanted to talk to Mom alone.

"What's up?" I asked Hal.

"You did it. I guess you really did it."

"What do you *mean?*"

"You remember that night Mom was explaining she's not supposed to sell houses in this part of town to Jewish people?"

"Uh—yeah. We were arguing about that clucky girl, Lyle, and how come Sidney was in our school."

"Well, you gave Miss Curmudgeon the impression that Izzy's family were our cousins. So she let them make an offer on this house. They're *not* our cousins, and they *are* Jewish. When the agency finds out, they're going to be pretty sore at Mom. They'll figure she must have known. When Sandra's parents find out, they'll probably have heart attacks!"

That was a nice idea and I laughed. Now that I thought about it, of course I remembered I used to walk Izzy to Hebrew school on Saturdays, him and Irvy.

"The thing is," I asked Hal, "how am I supposed to remember some kid is Jewish, when we're catching polliwogs or climbing a tree?"

15

New York

It's about six years now since we left Olcott Corners. After it was settled that the other Goodmans were really going to buy our house, Mom and Dad started talking about where we ought to live. Mom quit selling real estate. No one exactly said she had to, but she wanted to get out of that office. She wanted to leave Olcott, too, and so did I, and Dad was working too long hours to do all that commuting.

One day Mom hopped on the train and went into New York to look for apartments. She bought a new dress to do it in. She couldn't find one in our old part of town that she liked. Suddenly, without even going to look at it, she rented a summer place out on Long Island.

"You'll like anything with a beach and a boat, so what does it matter what it looks like?" she said.

"Yippee! A beach and a boat!" I started right in telling Jennifer all about oceans.

I was so excited about the summer that I practically forgot everything else. I worried some about how I could let Sidney know we'd moved, when I didn't even know where we'd be after the summer. Finally I decided I could call up Izzy when we were settled and tell him to get ahold of Sidney.

The only real wrench about leaving Olcott was when Mavis and Jennifer had to say good-bye. Jennifer bawled, and we all felt bad. We got to the beach, and it was just as good as I remembered, and Jennifer behaved well even without Mavis around.

At the end of the summer, when Mom was getting ready to go in and spend days looking at apartments, Dad came home and said he'd bought a co-op apartment down on Seventeenth Street. He said it was too good a buy to pass up, and too good an apartment. Mom almost died. I mean, she liked the apartment when she saw it, but she got cheated out of all that apartment-looking.

Hal went off to college and I settled into the public school. Except for not having much of any sports or playground, it was all right, and there were plenty of kids on my block to play with. In the city they play stickball, with a rubber ball and a broomstick, instead of baseball, but it's just about as good.

Once I called up Izzy and I told him where we were living and asked him to tell Sidney. He didn't know Sidney, though, and I guess he forgot.

I guess I forgot too. Then I went to Hughes High School, and most of my grade school friends went to other places. I was lonely, and all of a sudden I wanted to talk to Sidney, maybe because I'd been so lonely when I couldn't see him out in Olcott.

When you're a little kid, you think people you like will always be in your life. You don't realize you have to do anything about keeping track of them. So when I really wanted to see Sidney again, I grabbed the phone book. I wasn't scared of his mother anymore. There was no Martin Fine in the book for Olcott, though. I tried all the other suburban and even the city phone books. No Martin Fine anywhere. It hit me then I might never see him again, and I felt even lonelier than I had out in Olcott. This time I knew it was my own fault, and that didn't make things any better. Why hadn't I ever written him?

That day Sidney phoned me from Times Square, it was like a reprieve. Of course by then I had other friends at Hughes. Still, it was wonderful: I was so excited that I really had Sidney on the end of a phone again that I almost choked up.

173

I kept waiting for him to call again when he got back from New Jersey. I thought maybe we could get together pretty often. But he didn't call. Even thickheads like me wise up eventually, so one day I picked up the phone and got information to give me his phone number up in Hastings. It was a Saturday morning, and Mrs. Fine answered. I could tell it was her right away.

Of course, my voice had changed, and she didn't recognize it. She said, "Yes, Sidney's upstairs. Is that Jeff?"

I said, "No, it's me. Berries. Berries Goodman."

There was complete silence, and for a minute I thought she had hung up on me. Then Sidney answered, "Hello?"

"Hello, it's me, Berries."

"Oh—well, gee! What do you know?"

"Nothing much. How was New Jersey?"

"Oh, it was fine. Listen, what are you doing now?"

"Telephoning you, stupid."

"Thanks a bunch, stupid. I mean, what're you doing *today?*"

"Maybe I'll take a trip to Hastings. Are there trains?"

"Sure, that'd be great. I mean, I was thinking of coming in, but I've got to go to a dentist out here this afternoon. Look, the trains leave Grand Central at thirty-eight after the hour. You could get the eleven thirty-eight. I'll meet you at the station."

"O.K., here I come."

At the Hastings station, I decided I'd better find out how the land lay. "What's your mother going to say?" I asked Sidney.

"Maybe she'll have hysterics," he said airily. "Let's go home and see."

What Mrs. Fine did, of course, was just about what she did when I used to go home with Sidney years ago. She said, "Oh, hullo, Berries, come in. I was just making some coffee."

We sat down and had coffee and doughnuts, and she never mentioned anything about Olcott Corners. Sidney said something about me helping him to get the bus to New Jersey, and Mrs. Fine said, "You never told me you'd run into Berries in New York."

"I don't tell you everything, Mom, because I don't want you to worry." He was half kidding, half not. "Besides, I didn't run into him, I phoned him to come buy me a Coke."

Her eyes and Sidney's met for an instant, and then she turned to me and asked about my school. After a while she got up and said she had some shopping to do. We finished up the doughnuts and then went up to Sidney's room to play records. His diplomas and academic prizes were framed on the stairway. He shrugged one

175

shoulder. "Excuse my doting mother."

Up in his room he had a lot of wrestling trophies. I asked, "When did you get the wrestling bug?"

"When I didn't grow brawny enough for football and basketball. I'm going to be on the Olympic wrestling team."

"Are you now? I just want the Nobel Prize, if it's all right with you."

He got a wrestling hold on me, even though I'm a head taller and twenty pounds heavier, and I gave up.

"Are you all set for Harvard?" I asked.

"Nope. I got accepted. Everyone who gets accepted at Harvard goes there, so I decided I'd be different. I'm going to Carleton."

I lay on the floor and listened to the record a while, and then I said, "At first, when I called, I thought your mother had hung up on me. Did she act sore?"

"Not exactly. She was surprised, and she was sort of thinking about working up to a big scene, so I kidded her. That usually works the best. I just said my long-lost friend was coming to call, and did we have a Coke or something. Maybe she thinks you're less of a threat than Jeff, right now."

Sidney changed the record. "That was crazy, the way they wouldn't let us play together out in Olcott, after the accident. I can see now, I should never have told Mom about Sandra daring me to jump. Mom could never understand that's the way kids act. I must have been sort of a tattletale little kid, anyway."

"I told on Sandra finally. Then I kicked Mrs. Graham in the shins. That was good." I told Sidney all about that.

He said, "The trouble was, Mom couldn't see that your family were any different from Sandra's. If your mother had ever called up or anything . . ."

"I think she was afraid your mother would blow up at her."

We went down to the cellar to play ping-pong, and I remembered to ask him what happened to Sandra. He said she really did go bowling with Izzy. He didn't know whether Izzy's father took them, because by the time Sidney saw them, they were older and they were by themselves. Sidney said Sandra was winning, and I laughed. The next year she went off to boarding school. Sidney said, "I guess they just had to get her away from Izzy and that vulgar bowling alley!"

He went on. "I saw her again last summer—I was out in Olcott for a party. I even danced with her. She's pretty, but she's not too popular. She's awfully big and a lot of boys are scared of her. Not me, of course.

"She asked if I remembered falling at the culvert, and she said she didn't blame my mother for being so mad. I was sort of surprised she even mentioned it. And you know what?"

"What?"

"She's at Carleton." He added quickly, "That's not why I'm going, of course."

"Too bad I can't come too." I cut the ball so it almost bounced back over the net and won a point.

"You play lousy ping-pong," Sidney said, and he won the set. I said I'd better check the trains home pretty soon. I'd forgotten to tell my mother where I was going.

"She'll be surprised when I tell her," I said.

"Next time I'll come see you. Is the icebox still empty? I'll bring supplies. Have you still got Spooky and Jennifer?"

"Both going strong. You ought to see that Jennifer. She's a real brat. She fights with Mom all the time. Mom doesn't know how to handle her—Jennifer really needs someone to Mavis her."

I got home and told Mom where I'd been, and she was surprised, but for a funny reason. "I thought you'd forgotten all about Sidney," she said.

HARPER TROPHY BOOKS
you may enjoy reading

The Little House Books by *Laura Ingalls Wilder*

J1 Little House in the Big Woods
J2 Little House on the Prairie
J3 Farmer Boy
J4 On the Banks of Plum Creek
J5 By the Shores of Silver Lake
J6 The Long Winter
J7 Little Town on the Prairie
J8 These Happy Golden Years
J31 The First Four Years

J9 The Noonday Friends *by Mary Stolz*
J10 Look Through My Window *by Jean Little*
J11 Journey from Peppermint Stréet *by Meindert DeJong*
J12 White Witch of Kynance *by Mary Calhoun*
J14 Catch As Catch Can *by Josephine Poole*
J15 Crimson Moccasins *by Wayne Dyre Doughty*
J16 Gone and Back *by Nathaniel Benchley*
J17 The Half Sisters *by Natalie Savage Carlson*
J18 A Horse Called Mystery *by Marjorie Reynolds*
J19 The Seventeenth-Street Gang *by Emily Cheney Neville*
J20 Sounder *by William H. Armstrong*

J21 The Wheel on the School *by Meindert DeJong*
J22 The Secret Language *by Ursula Nordstrom*
J23 A Kingdom in a Horse *by Maia Wojciechowska*
J24 The Golden Name Day *by Jennie D. Lindquist*
J25 Hurry Home, Candy *by Meindert DeJong*
J26 Walk the World's Rim *by Betty Baker*
J27 Her Majesty, Grace Jones *by Jane Langton*
J28 Katie John *by Mary Calhoun*
J29 Depend on Katie John *by Mary Calhoun*
J30 Honestly, Katie John! *by Mary Calhoun*

J32 Feldman Fieldmouse *by Nathaniel Benchley*
J33 A Dog for Joey *by Nan Gilbert*
J34 The Walking Stones *by Mollie Hunter*
J35 Trapped *by Roderic Jeffries*
J36 The Grizzly *by Annabel and Edgar Johnson*
J37 Kate *by Jean Little*
J38 Getting Something on Maggie Marmelstein
     by Marjorie Weinman Sharmat
J39 By the Highway Home *by Mary Stolz*

J41 The Haunted Mountain *by Mollie Hunter*
J42 The Diamond in the Window *by Jane Langton*
J43 The Power of Stars *by Louise Lawrence*
J44 From Anna *by Jean Little*
J45 Apples Every Day *by Grace Richardson*
J46 Freaky Friday *by Mary Rodgers*
J47 Sarah and Katie *by Dori White*
J48 The Trumpet of the Swan *by E. B. White*

J49 Only Earth and Sky Last Forever *by Nathaniel Benchley*
J50 Dakota Sons *by Audree Distad*
J51 A Boy Called Fish *by Alison Morgan*
J52 If Wishes Were Horses *by Keith Robertson*
J53 In a Blue Velvet Dress *by Catherine Sefton*
J54 Game for Demons *by Ben Shecter*
J55 Charlotte's Web *by E. B. White*
J56 Stuart Little *by E. B. White*

J57 The Hotel Cat *by Esther Averill*
J58 Julie of the Wolves *by Jean Craighead George*
J59 The Witch of Fourth Street and Other Stories
     by Myron Levoy
J60 The Cabin on Ghostly Pond *by Marjorie Reynolds*

J62 The Mother Market *by Nancy Brelis*
J63 Hemi: a Mule *by Barbara Brenner*
J64 The Giant Under the Snow *by John Gordon*
J65 The Boyhood of Grace Jones *by Jane Langton*
J66 Bridget *by Gen LeRoy*
J67 Pilot Down, Presumed Dead *by Marjorie Phleger*
J68 Hog Wild! *by Julia Brown Ridle*
J69 Here Comes Herb's Hurricane! *by James Stevenson*
J70 Captains of the City Streets *by Esther Averill*
J71 Luvvy and the Girls *by Natalie Savage Carlson*
J72 Berries Goodman *by Emily Cheney Neville*
J73 It's Like This, Cat *by Emily Cheney Neville*

HARPER & ROW, PUBLISHERS, INC.
10 East 53rd Street, New York, New York 10022